MARIGUANO

Juan Ochoa

Texas Review Press
Huntsville, Texas

FIRST EDITION, 2013
Requests for permission to reproduce material from this work should be
sent to:

Permissions
Texas Review Press
English Department
Sam Houston State University
Huntsville, TX 77341-2146

Library of Congress Cataloging-in-Publication Data

Ochoa, Juan, 1966-
  Mariguano / Juan Ochoa.
    pages cm
    ISBN 978-1-937875-32-9 (pbk. : alk. paper)
    1. Elections--Mexico--Fiction. 2. Drug traffic--Mexico--Fiction.
    3. Corruption--Mexico--Fiction. 4. Mexico--Politics and govern-
    ment--Fiction. I. Title.
    PS3615.C45M37 2013
    813'.6--dc23

                                        2013013295

To my wife, Tila, my lover, my best and oftentimes only friend, for all the precious moments we spent apart while working on this novel. To my daughters, Joy, Desi, and Amy porque quiero que sepan lo mucho que las quiero.

MARIGUANO

Chapter I

I have a family, mom, dad, brothers, a sister, just like everyone else. I'm raised in a decent house that doesn't tolerate foul language or lies, and I have to take my plate to the sink after I eat. But I also have my Old Man and his *clicka*. When I was thirteen, my Old Man taught me how to drive, take tequila shots, and shoot out of a moving vehicle all in one sitting. My dad's not the only one teaching me things, though. I have five or six guys around at all times making sure I get things straight.

Whenever we get a big score, I have to sit in a hotel room with one of my Old Man's men counting the money over and over. I complained once and el Chaparro said, "Chato, someday you'll do a deal and not go crazy and try to grab more than your share because your dad was smart enough to make you sick of counting money." I learn all kinds of things from these guys, like always be wary of the kindness of strangers and never trust a guy who says, "Trust me." I know better than to front something that I can't afford to lose, and I'll never steal or put the finger on anyone. Just that alone is enough to keep a guy alive for a long time, but I can figure out other things, too. I've learned to read a newspaper better than a stockbroker. I know that if there's an article about someone losing a load or getting busted I'll be holed up somewhere waiting by the phone for at least two calls: one from the guy wanting to *arreglar la bronca* and get out of jail and another from some cop looking to sell a load of drugs cheap. I know that if there's an article announcing a new *comandante* coming to town we'll be throwing a party complete with mariachis and whores to baptize President Reagan's newest godson—that's what my Old Man calls cops, *ahijados de Reagan*. I can tell if I'm going to be holed up waiting for a phone call or getting laid that day just by reading the headlines.

In the summer of 1983, the story taking up all the headlines has nothing to do with us, but I learn a lot from it anyway. There are two major newspapers in Reynosa. *Las Noticias* is owned and edited by Don Félix Tarta. Don Beto Garrado publishes *El Día* and an evening edition called *La Noche*. Don Félix also owns a radio station. Each paper dedicates a few columns to editorials denouncing its rival as an *amarillista* rag. *El Día* is supposedly more powerful than *Las Noticias*, but I really can't see how since everyone in town buys both papers and believes neither one.

Don Beto and Don Félix are also rivals in the public transport business. Each man owns a line of *peseras*. *Peseras* are like little buses that take people all around town for a peso. Only they're not buses. They're beat up cargo vans with bald tires and shitty brakes. There are no seats in these vans other than the driver's. Passengers sit on milk crates that topple over every time the driver takes a sharp turn. All of Don Beto's vans are painted yellow. Don Félix's vans are also yellow but with a red stripe, so they're called *franja rojas*.

The drivers of the yellow vans are having a war with the drivers of the *franja roja* vans over the routes they drive; the newspapers call it *La guerra de las peseras*, the Pesera Wars. Each side claims that the other is cutting into their routes. Vans are getting burned out left and right. Lately, you can't open a newspaper without seeing the picture of a driver who's been beaten or shot to death next to a torched van. The Pesera Wars are selling a lot of newspapers.

Mom, Dad, Raulito and I have been staying at the Hotel El Camino in Reynosa for most of the summer. Mom and my Old Man stay in room 324 and Raulito and I are in 325—Mom says it doesn't look right for kids to be alone in a hotel without a parent near. When the fair's in town, it's not that bad in Reynosa because we can spend all night at the *Palenque* then sleep through the next day. The *Palenque's* real cool especially now that Vicente has been bringing his sister-in-law to see the headliners during the *variedad*. I've seen a lot of pretty girls, and even been with a few, but they're nothing in comparison with Cynthia. It's hard to describe sitting in sweltering heat watching two cocks slash the shit out of each other surrounded by the finest pieces of ass in Reynosa, and then comes this princess of something and all that beauty goes away. Cynthia is something royal sitting daintily with her legs crossed at the ankles fanning herself with a *lotería* card—I don't know the words, but the type of sweet wholesome girl who could scar a guy for life.

When we don't go to the cockfights and are just in our rooms with nothing but Mexican TV to watch, Raulito and I go out of our minds with boredom. To keep from fighting over what to watch and making Mom mad by waking her before noon, Raulito and I came up with a game we call *pesera* roulette.

First we do a round of rock paper scissors to see who gets to pick the van. Raulito likes Don Beto's yellow vans, but I always go for the underdog and pick Don Félix's *franja roja* vans. Once we board a van, we squat near the driver and the door. Most of the time, we just cruise around in the *pesera* getting crotch shots from the girls who topple off their milk crates. But every now and then, a rival van will close in and we have to move our asses out of the van quick before we get caught in the middle of a torching. Fucking Raulito is only twelve and can already hit the ground running from a moving van without tripping.

Raulito and I are just about to get on a *franja roja pesera* in front of our hotel when Vicente and his cousin Arturo pull up in a bad ass Custom Chevy Van. Vicente, or Vicente el Loco as everyone calls him, is the right hand man of the chief of the municipal police in Reynosa. Vicente stands as tall as my dad but looks smaller because he's thinner. His sun washed face is slender and his nose, cheeks, and chin are hard and elegant. He looks like a Mexican Peter Fonda and even has a habit of slicking his hair down with his hand like Fonda does in *Easy Rider*.

The van is brown with four captain's chairs and a bench seat in the back. It has carpeting all the way up the walls and even on the headliner. The dash and a console between the driver and passenger seat are trimmed in wood. The stereo and speakers have been ripped out leaving raw holes, but other than that the van is cherry.

Vicente lowers the electric window and says, "Your dad told me to come get you."

I grin. "Are we going by your house?" All summer, I've been inventing excuses to drop by Vicente's house and see Cynthia.

"You'd like that wouldn't you *cabrón*." Vicente punches the van before Raulito and I are in our seats and we fall over each other. "We're going to Los Ramones to call on one of your dad's *compadres*."

"Which one?"

"I heard your dad say his *compadre* Lolo." Arturo says it like he's giving testimony. That's how all these fuckers around my Old Man talk. No one knows a fucking thing except what they're told. That's another thing I've learned from hanging around my Old Man: never give up any more information than you have to.

Arturo's turned in his seat facing us. He's a huge fucker. I'd say 280 pounds, maybe three something, but it's all big, dark, hairy Mexican. Arturo isn't any kind of a cop like his cousin, so he can't carry a gun. He doesn't need one.

"We're picking up an ice chest, some Topo Chico, and a bottle of Buchanan's." Arturo loves to drink. Arturo smiles. It's a big toothy smile that appears through the slit in his beard.

"So, we're going to a *parranda*?"

Arturo looks at Vicente then back at me and says, "Your dad said to find you guys then pick up a bottle of Buchanan's."

On the street ahead of us, two of Don Beto's yellow vans block in a *franja roja* driver. Four guys barrel out of one of the yellow vans and drag the driver of the *franja roja* out of his seat and into the street. They circle the fallen driver kicking and stomping him. A guy carrying a gas can gets off the other yellow van and starts dousing the *franja roja* as the passengers fall over each other trying to get off the *pesera*.

"Aren't you going to do something about those guys?" I ask Vicente.

"That's no longer my jurisdiction." Vicente laughs. He hands me a post-card sized laminated badge that says he's a commissioned agent, level C, of the *Seguridad Nacional Federal*. This badge is what's known as a *charola*. The word translates to "platter," I guess because of the size and shape of the badge, but it's really a license to do what ever the fuck you want. I've never heard of the *Seguridad Nacional*, but then again there's a new law enforcement agency popping up or shutting down every other day so it's hard to keep track.

"Give me a cigarette, Arturo." Out the back window the *franja roja* van goes up in flames. I smoke.

We pick up my Old Man and Onésimo near the bridge. My Old Man is getting his boots shined while he talks to Domingo Gonzálo, Reynosa's chief of police. Gonzálo wears a Colt .45 with gold grips and has a couple of uniformed cops hanging around with him. They try to look tough in front of their *jefe*, but I can tell they're all afraid of my Old Man. My Old Man, like always, is sporting his best handwoven Panama and is decked out in a Mexican leisure suit called a *conjunto.* His tailored shirt hangs just low enough around his waist to conceal the gold and silver engraved grips of his .38 Colt Super. He stands a tall thick frame and dresses out at about 220, copper skin, finely trimmed mustache a la Clark Gable, every stitch of clothing perfectly fit and matched all the way down to his handmade ostrich boots. Just because Gonzálo is chief doesn't mean he's in charge. My Old Man is the baddest motherfucker in the Valley, and when he's around, everyone else is second.

Onésimo is Vicente el Loco's younger brother and my Old Man's current right hand man. He's tall and stout, bigger than his older brother and is great at picking up chicks.

After a squabble, Onésimo takes the wheel. Vicente rides next to me in one of the captain's chairs. Raulito and Arturo sit on the bench seat at the back of the van. We have an ice chest and a case of mineral water. Except for Raulito, we're all drinking whiskey highballs.

"*Mi vieja* got pissed when she saw me taking the glasses, *compadre,*" Onésimo says.

"My *comadre* doesn't want you to drink?" My Old Man is fumbling around with a bank bag. He always carries some kind of bag. He opens the bank bag and starts lining .38 Super clips on the dashboard. My old Man carries at least seven extra clips in his bag. He keeps two more clips in sheaths looped on his belt. Counting the clip in his gun, that makes ten clips or nearly two boxes of shells. My Old Man says if you're going to lose a gunfight it should be *por falta de huevos,* not for lack of bullets. It's a cool saying. He counts his clips one more time then puts them back into the bag.

"*No, compadre, mi vieja* couldn't care less about me drinking." Onésimo holds up his glass. "I take her glasses and forget to bring them back. She said the kids are drinking straight from the faucet because I haven't left a glass in the house."

Los Ramones, my Old Man's home town, is in the state of Nuevo León. It's less than a couple of hundred kilometers from Reynosa but the road is so bad and heavy with camion traffic that the trip takes hours. There's a checkpoint thirty kilometers out of Reynosa on the state line between Tamaulipas and Nuevo León. This checkpoint is called La Treinta. Americans who want to take their vehicles any further south than this point have to get a tourist visa and a temporary import sticker for their cars. The checkpoint is set up to stop contraband and stolen vehicles from going further south. Our van is stolen.

We pull up under a concrete awning and Onésimo gets out of the van and starts shaking hands with the officers on duty. They are *Registro Federal de Vehículos* agents and Customs agents known as *aduanales*. Onésimo is a *Registro* agent, but he is on leave so he can work for my dad. My Old Man is out of the van shaking hands with some *aduanales* and slipping wads of money in their breast pockets. These guys cheer and hug on my Old Man every time we pass this checkpoint. Guys cheer and hug on my Old Man at every checkpoint we go through.

My Old Man gets back in the van and says, "My *compadre* Lolo hasn't been through here in days." He turns in his seat, snaps his fingers, and points to the bottle of whiskey. Arturo, Vicente, and I race to pick up the bottle to fix him another drink. Vicente ends up pouring the whiskey while Arturo adds the ice and soda. I hold the glass. My Old Man takes his drink and says, "*Pinche* Lolo must be hiding out in McAllen."

So this is it. When we left Reynosa, I thought we were just out for a little party on wheels. But now it's clear that we're going to see Lolo to pick him up for a "*levantón.*" I'm not surprised by the news. My Old Man helped Lolo get started in the *falluca* business, contraband business. Lolo's done real well for himself and expanded his organization to a small fleet of vans since then, but he hasn't thrown so much as a thank you our way. We're between jobs right now and times are tough but not for Lolo and my Old Man's offended. Being successful at something is the worst thing a Mexican can do to another Mexican.

My Old Man has had me making calls to Lolo, but every time I try to connect, Lolo is out or just left, expected to return soon, asleep, in the bathroom, and so on. My Old Man doesn't like it when people dodge his calls.

Lolo hadn't passed through La Treinta so he's not going to be at home, but we're still heading for Los Ramones. Onésimo looks in the rearview mirror and says to Vicente, "You see Loco, see how easy we got through that checkpoint with me driving? All those guys lined up as soon as they saw it was me." Onésimo hands back his glass and gives me a wink. I fix him another whiskey highball.

Onésimo says to my Old Man, "When I worked in *El Registro*, I was in charge of all those *cabrones* and I always gave them their fair cut. *Pinche* Vicente thinks he could have gotten us through the checkpoint with his *Seguridad Nacional charola*. That fucking agency is so new its own director doesn't know it exists."

"At least I have a badge, you disgraced parking attendant," Vicente shoots back. "That's the hardest thing for *Registro* agents to do, *compadre*," Vicente says to my Old Man. "Parking the cars they confiscate. They can't figure out the gears. They keep putting them in R for *rápido*."

My Old Man lowers his window, looks down the sights of his Colt Super, and shoots a horse that is grazing on the side of the road. Through my window, I follow the wounded animal as it limps away until it falls, turning into to a dark spot with a pumping neck that grows smaller and smaller and is too far behind us for me to see. Onésimo starts to sing a song he learned at the Plaza Garibaldi when he was in Mexico City fixing his leave from the *Registro*.

Onésimo is a good singer and the song he brought from Plaza Garibaldi suits his voice. It's a love ballad called *"El Ramalazo."* He sings about a guy who loved a woman under his favorite tree or something like that. But when she broke up with him, he chopped the tree down, and the crashing timber fell so hard that even his heart ached.

Onésimo hangs on "*Corazón*" during the chorus. I like this song.

We pull into Los Ramones well after dark. My Old Man tells Onésimo to cruise around the *plaza* a couple of times. He takes his foot off the gas and lets the van idle around the *plaza* as we check out men loitering on park benches or leaning on the walls of cantinas across the street. We pull up in front of Chema's Cantina. My Old Man dips his chin towards a tall lanky weather-beaten man wearing a longsleeve denim shirt, standing in front of the bar with four other guys. Vicente swings open the side door and he and Arturo spill out of the van. Vicente draws his gun. Arturo rushes the men standing on the corner and knocks down two guys as he tears through the group. Onésimo is out of the van with his gun leveled at the ones left standing.

"I'm looking for Fidencio," Onésimo says. There's a funny thing about a *levantón*. Whenever it becomes clear who is actually getting picked up, there's a combined reaction of dread and relief. I see the tall man's knees buckle and a wave of doom cover his face when Onésimo says Fidencio's name. The guys who are with Fidencio, though, beam with delight once they figure out that it's their buddy who's the target of this raid and not them.

Vicente moves in next to the tall man and buries his gun into his ribs. "*No te hagas pendejo, we know who you are.*"

Fidencio throws his hands up. "*Señor, se lo juro.* I have no idea why you'd want to waste your time with me."

Fidencio begins to sway. Vicente grabs his arm and moves him over to the van. My Old Man lowers his window and says, "*Perdón caballero,* I was just wondering if you could give me directions to La Hacienda San Antonio?"

Fidencio's knees buckle for a second time, then he rights himself. He turns to the men he was standing with moments earlier and says, "You sorry sons of bitches. Not one of you offered a word in my defense." We all laugh.

"Julio, I swear I thought I was a dead man when I saw this *muchacho* pull his gun." Fidencio's riding in my seat with Vicente next to him. I sit on the bench seat with my little brother and Arturo. My Old Man's turned in his seat facing Fidencio and is still laughing.

"What'd you think when you saw my men, Fidencio: 'I wonder what goat cried rape?'" He wipes tears from his eyes.

"It had to be that spotted goat, I thought," Fidencio says taking the drink I prepared for him. "She's the biggest gossip in the whole flock."

We drive out of Los Ramones down a rutted road past the cemetery. I know the road. It leads to the hacienda and the three walls of the adobe hut where my father was born. As a child, I spent a summer here chopping down *maize* with a machete on my tío Raúl's land. I remember it being hot and miserable.

At Fidencio's place we all get out and take pisses. My dad and Fidencio go off to one side and talk. They stand facing each other in the moonlight—the sounds of the night cloaking their words save for an occasional *carcajada*. My Old Man throws an arm around Fidencio and they return to where we're standing. "We're going to load some sheep," my Old Man says.

Fidencio stands holding the gate. Vicente and Raulito are in the pen chasing sheep. Vicente grabs one by the ears and steers it toward the gate while Raulito pushes. Fidencio lets the animal pass, and I grab it by the head and pull. Arturo wraps his arms around the sheep and lifts. With Arturo carrying the hind quarters and me steering, the sheep runs on its front legs into our van. We do this six times. My Dad tells us to pull the sheeps' legs out from under them and we get them to lie down between our seats in the back of the van.

"There isn't room for any more?" my Old Man asks getting into his seat.

I have my feet on a sheep's stomach holding her down. "If we leave the ice chest, maybe we could fit one more."

"No, we're not drinking straight whiskey," my Old Man says. "Straight whiskey will make a man do stupid things. Always remember that *mi'jo*." He shakes Fidencio's hand through his open window. "*Bueno* Fidencio, it was good seeing you again. Say hello to your brother León for me."

"My brother León has been dead for more than ten years."

"I know," my Old Man says. "The way you looked back in town, I'd say you're about due for a family reunion."

"I think I can put it off if I avoid *chistosos* like you." Fidencio lays his hand on my Old Man's arm. "You take care of yourself, Julio."

My Old Man shoves a few wadded up bills into Fidencio's breast pocket.

"Go buy yourself a few dances with those fat bitches at Chema's." My Old man cocks his thumb to the sheep in the back of the van and says, "I know it must be hard saying goodbye to your girlfriends like this." Then the smile flies off my Old Man's face and his voice turns to the tone he uses when I'm late running an errand, a low rumbling from down deep, and the hair on the back of my neck prickles as he says, "You tell Lolo I have a name, Don Julio Cortina, and he and everyone else has to respect that name."

Fidencio nods and has to lick his lips before he can say, "*Adiós*."

We drive over the rutted road past the cemetery and back around the *plaza* in Los Ramones. My Old Man makes Onésimo stop so he can shake hands with guys still hanging around. He shows off the sheep and describes the look on Fidencio's face to all the men he greets. I recognize some of these guys. Some work for Lolo. Some are related to me. The sheep are shitting and pissing all over place. Before we leave the *plaza*, my Old Man empties his Colt Super into a stop sign.

"Why'd we take Fidencio's sheep, Dad?" I ask.

"Fidencio's never owned anything but a hangover all his life." My Old Man hands me back his glass. "These sheep belong to Lolo. So does this van. I got the police chief to pick it up." My Old Man takes a long pull from his whiskey and says to no one in particular, "Make sure Gonzálo gets two sheep."

On the highway back to Reynosa, Onésimo looks at his brother through the rearview mirror. "You think your *Seguridad Nacional* badge can keep a rustling charge off our back, Vicente? *La Policía Rural* might be out tonight." Onésimo hands me back his glass.

"I hope we do get stopped." Vicente scoops up a handful of ice and rubs it over a sheep's asshole then dumps the ice into Onésimo's glass. "I'm not going to pull my badge until they have you strung up for deflowering virgin wool."

Onésimo takes his glass and drinks. He winces and takes another drink. "Don't think I don't know what you're doing, *pinche* Loco," Onésimo says spitting out bits of sheep shit. Onésimo drinks in big gulps then starts to sing "*El Ramalazo*" over the bleating of the sheep.

We drive through the night. The sheep piss and shit all the way back to Reynosa. The morning sun shines purple on the cottonball bellies of the overcast clouds. I hang my head out the window trying to escape the stench. The burned-out hull of a *pesera* smolders in the morning light as we cruise into Reynosa's still sleepy streets. There's a dark purplish stain next to the *pesera* skeleton, but I don't focus on that.

"Look at the sky," I say to no one in particular.

Arturo says, "*Cielo de terciopelo al amanecer,*" without looking out the window.

"A velvet morning?" I ask, surprised at Arturo's choice of words.

"Yeah, I've seen thousands. But never when I'm straight."

It was a fun night. Vicente kept sticking his finger up the sheep's ass then stirring Onésimo's drink. Onésimo sang. And I could even sneak a smoke every now and then. We drive through town to El Café Rey and leave the sheep locked in the van while we go in for breakfast. I wipe the shit off my boots then follow my Old Man into the café. I order some huevos rancheros and a beer. The little bell on the door rings and a very light complexioned elderly man with dyed jet-black hair comes shuffling in. Vicente elbows me and says, "That's the owner of *Las Noticias.*"

Not two minutes later, the bell rings again and another old man comes in, only this guy is a little fatter and is balding. "That's Don Beto, from *El Día*," Arturo says over a plate of chorizo and eggs.

"El Johnny only uses a newspaper to roll marijuana on," my Old Man says and the whole table laughs.

The owners of Reynosa's two leading newspapers hug each other in greeting then sit down for breakfast across the café from our table. My Old Man calls the waiter over and tells him to put their orders on our tab: "Tell them Don Julio Cortina is inviting them to breakfast this morning." My Old Man gives our table a wink and says, "Maybe I'll get my name in the papers."

Outside the sidewalks begin to swell with people flagging down *peseras* to take them to work. Before we leave the café, I have to wait with pen ready while my Old Man shakes hands with Don Beto and Don Félix and gets the addresses where I'll be delivering each of them a sheep.

Chapter II

My Old Man moves us out of the Hotel El Camino in Reynosa and across the Rio Grande to San Juan, Texas so my little brother and I can start school. We rent two one-bedroom apartments near la Virgen de San Juan Basilica—it got upgraded from a Shrine after some Protestant went kamikaze on the original church with a crop-dusting plane filled with gas. The one surviving artifact that didn't burn was a bust of the Virgin. The apartments are only a little bigger than our rooms at the hotel but they have central air and that's really all that matters when looking for a place in the Valley.

I have to decide what I'm going to do. I can move back to east Texas to a little town called Ben Wheeler, where we lived before my mom decided to follow my Old Man to the Valley. They can't be apart from each other for too long before Mom starts accusing Dad of blowing his money on his *compadres* and Dad starts figuring that Mom is fucking every guy she meets—they are both right. My folks are still paying on the east Texas house and ten acres. But finishing my senior year at a redneck high school that gives me swats for waving to a white cheerleader during class isn't worth my Old Man giving me grief over the added expenses.

I have that Reynosa girl, Cynthia, to think about, too. We aren't officially *novios* but we still go out to the movies every Sunday. Right from the start with Cynthia, she makes it clear that she is a *señorita* and that for now we are only "*pretendientes.*" My Old Man tells me that *pretendiente* means she is trying to trap me into marrying her and I should stay away. I think Cynthia has an ass that is worth marrying.

I can get my GED and skip my senior year, but then I'll have to find a job and a place to live. The only work experience I have is fast food and running errands for my Old Man. I can join the Marines like my brother Rubén did. At least I'd have a place to stay. But the Marines are too much like Rubén, loud and ignorant. I'd rather join the Navy so I can travel to Singapore, Bangkok, anywhere far. But fucking Rubén and everyone else in the family will call me a *joto* for wearing the little sailor suit.

In the end, it's weed that makes up my mind. Because I've been working with my Old Man, I haven't had any weed for most of the summer: I can help him sell the shit out of weed, but if he catches me smoking any pot my ass is kicked faster than a rabbit gets fucked. Aside from school, I don't have anywhere to score for weed without my Old Man catching on. This is my third high school since entering ninth grade. I was always able to score for weed in every other school. I don't figure the high school in San Juan to be any different.

I wait until Mom gets the coffee and eggs in front of my Old Man before I break the news about finishing my senior year in the Valley.

"I was going to use you in a couple of days, but I can find someone else," my Old Man says from behind his copy of *El Día.*

"Do you even know where the school is?" My mom takes a seat next to my Old Man. Mom wears a robe that matches her nightgown and walks around the house like she's expecting Robin Leach and the film crew of *Lifestyles of the Rich and Famous* to come rolling up our drive. "It's across the tracks on I-Road. Straight down, just a few blocks from the H.E.B. where we buy groceries."

"I've got most of my credits already, so I probably don't have to take that many classes," I say.

"You've got your ID, right?"

I check my wallet and dig out a worn Certificate of Registered Birth and my driver's license. Behind a school picture of Raulito, I also have my Social Security card. The whole record of my existence fits in my wallet.

"So, what do you want, lunch money or something?" my mom asks. "I need to pay the bills." She's looking at my dad. "And a bigger place or I'll just go crazy. You can't have anyone over it's so small. And Luordes called and said *la niña* has been asking for grandma to buy her a dress."

"He didn't give me my fucking change from the paper this morning, *qué fea pinche maña*." My Old Man drops his fork on his plate. "If you say you're going to fucking school, go to fucking school."

"No, but if you need me in a couple of days . . ."

"And what the fuck can you do for me other than drive? Do you got a client? A connection? There's a thousand *pendejos* I can call for the good you do me. Go to fucking school already." My Old Man hacks at his eggs like he's cutting coke.

My mom says, "If you can't go out with your dad, maybe you can get a job after school. There're a lot bodegas around. Go bag some grapefruit or something."

"Working for scraps," my Old Man barks. "*Hazte pendejo en la escuela* and leave the work for the men."

"You're one to be talking about working for scraps," my mom says. "All I ever hear around here is a suitcase full, a trunk full, a *pinche* Cessna. If you can make so much on a suitcase full of junk, why not a whole truckload or train cars, something big like that?"

"Are you going to start with that shit again?" my Old Man says throwing the fork into his eggs.

"The more you move, the bigger the chance of getting caught!"

"If I were a man, I wouldn't be scared. I wouldn't be working for peanuts," Mom says waiving him off.

My Old Man looks at me like I just ran a red light with a trunk full of weed and says, "What the fuck are you doing standing there? Get your ass to school already."

I find my way to the front office and tell the lady behind the counter that I want to enroll. She doesn't freak out that my parents aren't with me like they did at my other schools up north. While I fill out a few forms—with MIGRANT stamped on top—the lady has my grades faxed over from my old school. Turns out I only need to take four classes to have enough credits to graduate.

I work out my schedule where I leave school by one o'clock. My last class is a split Government and U.S. History course. The Government part of the class meets before lunch and the History part meets after. By the third day of school, a kid from class comes up to me during lunch and says, "You drive that red Mustang with the white top."

"The '67, yeah."

"Is it a convertible?"

"Nah, it's just got a white vinyl top."

"*Está de aquéllas.*"

"Thanks."

"I've got a joint. If you give me a ride home after class, I'll smoke it with you."

By the end of the month, I know where to score for the best *guatos*—that's what lids are called here—in Pharr, San Juan, and Alamo.

The kids in school are pretty cool for the most part even if they do call the teachers "el Sir" and "la Miss." There are jocks, a few guys in FFA jackets, geeks, freaks in black, rock 'n rollers, and the preppy bunch like in every other school. But here, they're all Mexican like me. There are a few white kids, and I thought I saw a black girl—it could have been a dark Mexican—but mostly all the kids are *raza*. And nobody gives a fuck if you get high. At my other schools, the stoners were considered good for laughs in class but they weren't someone you wanted to be seen with in the street. In the Valley, getting high is no big deal. The only thing I saw dividing the kids into cliques was money, who had what, but that's nothing. That's the way it is everywhere.

I have a car and my Old Man keeps me in loose change, so I make friends quick. Guys pull out joints in exchange for a cruise in my Mustang all the time. It isn't long before my Old Man catches wind to what I'm up to and pulls me in by making me meet him in Reynosa every day after school.

I have to be home by 1:15—the phone rings right at that time and if I'm not there to pick it up by the third ring, I get my ass chewed off. I drop off my books, get instructions, and turn around and go to Reynosa to run errands. My Old Man has us set up in La Majada, a *cabrito al pastor* restaurant that sits right up against the international bridge. I wait by the phone at La Majada and take messages for my Old Man. Right now all we're doing is fixing things with the *aduanales* in Mexican Customs for *falluqueros* to bring in loads of contraband like whiskey, perfumes, electronics, all that shit. If it fits on the bridge and you want to bring it into México without paying the high taxes, my Old Man is the man to see. I do the leg work, running to the bridge to guide vans through, talking to *comandantes*, shit like that. We're only filling in the gaps while we wait for real work: we got a load of weed we're fixing to bring up from Nayarit as soon as we figure out the transport. The food is good—everything gets put on a tab which nobody bothers us for because we help the restaurant's owner bring in contraband cooking supplies from the U.S.—and the times I have to go out and hand deliver a message to some *policía* or *aduanal*, I can steal away for a moment and see Cynthia.

Going off on my own like that chaps my Old Man's ass. He likes for everyone who works for him to be there the second he needs them. Except for el Chaparro and a few others, no one lasts very long working for my Old Man. Vicente has a full time job with the cops, so we can't count on him. Onésimo's on leave from his job, but he likes to whore around a lot, so he's not reliable. Fuck, most of the guys who work with my Old Man have one vice or another and disappear on a binge every time we make a score. Another reason my Old Man stays pissed all the time is that there's always some motherfucker not doing what he's supposed to do. I usually top that list.

El Chaparro is a *borracho*. And he's a sneaky fucking drunk at that. He looks at me with teddy bear button eyes, lips puckered like a dried prune, laughing enough to shake his whole body. Short stocky motherfucker plays all innocent just to come up with excuses to drink like, "Maybe we should have a few whiskeys while we wait for the *comandante*, just to keep loose. Not be all tense where he might think he can bully us into paying more." It's fucking hilarious. I don't give a fuck whose shift it is, no fucking *aduanal* ever tries to shake us down for more money. My Old Man would slap them around like stepchildren if they tried anything like that, but fucking Chaparro still pulls his bit.

El Chaparro has known me even before I was born. He met my folks when they were still boyfriend and girlfriend picking cotton in Weslaco. He was on the run back then for killing some fucker who was starting trouble in his native Veracruz. I don't know exactly what kind of shit because el Chaparro only refers to this guy as, "*Un necio que andaba chingando la madre por allí.*" Whatever this guy did, it bugged el Chaparro enough for him to fire a shotgun into his face. That was el Chaparro's first.

At school they're starting to talk about some test called the ACT. This kid brings it up in class and is able to say it's in Harlingen before the teacher shuts him up. Another time, I'm standing in the snack bar line and I hear these girls say that the

ACT is to get into college and it costs thirty-five bucks. It's a college entrance exam. I want to see if I can pass it. Just to see if I can. Christmas is six weeks away, and the test isn't until spring, so I can save thirty-five dollars by then. College is at least four years, and I don't know how much it costs, but I know it's expensive. I just want to see if I can pass the entrance exam, and that's all.

I sit with el Chaparro at La Majada. He's talked me into too many drinks, and I let my tongue go loose about the ACT and college. El Chaparro knows his shit. He's been a soldier, a boxer, done time in Laredo's infamous La Loma prison, been *primer capataz* in Reynosa's prison. Hell, el Chaparro's done time in Leavenworth. El Chaparro knows his shit. I have to remember to check myself so I don't fall for his shit.

" 'Course you're going to take that test." El Chaparro palms the table. He never slams his hand down on the table when he wants to make a point like my Old Man does. "When I met your Old Man, he was strutting around like the cock of the walk at the farm in Weslaco." El Chaparro hovers over his drink. "Your mom had just given birth to Isidro. Julio was proud of his son even though your *abuelita* said it wasn't his. Then little Chilo got sick. He needed to be put in an incubator. It cost $600. That was a lot of money back then. We were pulling field hand wages *en la cebolla*. Twenty-five cents a bucket." El Chaparro reaches over and pulls on the back of my neck till his head is rubbing on mine and then he drains half his drink. "Everyone in the camp was staying clear of your dad because they knew he needed money."

"They thought he was going to hit them up?"

"Damn right. He could clear out a bunkhouse faster than *la migra*. I see your dad about to go crazy trying to find money to pay for your big brother's hospital bill. Just when I think he's going to do something stupid, I see him bully this guy into giving him a ride. What the hell was that guy's name?"

"Where was my Old Man going?" I've heard this story hundreds of times, but I like the way el Chaparro tells it. "I see him get into the car, and like a gringo's dog, I jump into the back seat."

"Did you guys go knock off a liquor store?"

"No. You go to jail for that. We headed to this black church, just as it's letting out from mass—*los negritos* always put on their finest to go to church. We pull up, and Julio jumps out with a two-by-four. *Zaz!* He gets this big one, right across the head. I pull him into the back seat and pick him clean—wallet, chains, rings, his hat. I got a really nice hat." El Chaparro pauses reflectively and then starts looking for a waiter.

"What's the guy who's driving doing all this time?"

"Him? He's shitting all over himself. We got a *negrito* with a cracked head in the back seat! We dump the *negrito* and start to figure the take and Julio says, '*Falta*. Turn around so I can get another.'" El Chaparro laughs until tears stream from his eyes. "The driver starts begging us to take his car. Then he promises to sign over his paycheck if we just let him drive back to the camp. What the hell was that guy's name?"

"And did he do it?"

"Did he do it? We got back to camp and he went around telling everyone what we had done, and next thing you know, every guy in camp is signing over their check." El Chaparro clamps his stubby fingers over my hand and says, "I knew then that your Old Man was a man, a real one, one who'd do anything for his family. You're going to take that test, and you're going to pass, Chato."

"And then I'm going to get up the next day and take messages for my Old Man." I down what's left of my whiskey highball.

"Then you're going to go to college and get a job, wear a suit," el Chaparro says tugging on his collar. "Learn how to rob with a pen instead of a two-by-four, Chato. You're going to do something with your life. You can't be in *la movida* with us forever. You have to go become a lawyer or something, so you can get me and your Old Man out of *pedos*."

"A fucking lawyer, oh fuck, that's even more college."

"So, who cares? You're young. You've got time."

"How the fuck am I going to pay for college?" The little bell on the door jingles and a crippled midget crutches his way into the restaurant. He hands the cashier one of those plastic shopping bags they sell at the Mercado and it's loaded with coins. The midget begs on the bridge and brings in his take to the restaurant to exchange the coins for folding money. Then he rides home in a brand new car.

"Let us worry about paying for college, Chato. You just study. Guys with degrees never go to jail no matter how much they steal." El Chaparro orders another round of whiskey highballs.

The bell on the door jingles again and my Old Man walks into La Majada with Onésimo following close behind.

"Hey, Julio, what was that guy's name when we got the hat off that *negrito*?" el Chaparro asks raising his drink in greeting.

My Old Man takes a seat at our table and throws the newspaper he's carrying over to el Chaparro. "Never mind that nickel and dime shit. We have news from your home state, Chorty. My *compadre* Nacho sent me that newspaper. We just picked it up at the bus station."

I look over el Chaparro's shoulder and read the headlines from *El Tiempo de Veracruz*: "*Las calles se convierten en ríos de sangre, matan a Felipe Lagunilla*"—Streets Turn into Rivers of Blood, Felipe Lagunilla Has Been Killed. Felipe's cousin is the governor of Veracruz. I know Felipe Lagunilla personally; we get a lot of pot from him. El Chaparro looks up from the newspaper and asks, "Are we going?"

My Old Man drains my drink and says, "I'm going. You're going to Nayarit like we planned."

"What should I do, Dad?"

"Go home and get my shit together," my Old Man says, handing me some money. "Every spare clip you can find in the house and stop off at *la tienda de la curva* in Hidalgo and buy me as many boxes of .38 Super shells as you can."

"Then what do I do?"

"Then you go home and wait for me, c*hingada madre mi'jo*, I just told you that."

"No, I mean do I get my stuff together too? Am I going with you to Veracruz?"

"Just do what I fucking told you and get your ass home." My Old Man heads for the office behind the cashier's stand so he can use the phone.

El Chaparro grabs me by the arm and stops me before I leave our table. "You go home and study for that test. Leave this mess for us. When I get back from Nayarit, you won't have to worry about how to pay for college or anything else for a while." El Chaparro winks his teddy bear button eye and points at the newspaper and asks, "What do you see?"

"I see Felipe lying dead in the street."

"That's what you see. I see a guy whose cousin isn't governor anymore. You go home and study for that test. Not everything we do ends in laughs."

I leave the restaurant and haul ass across the bridge back into the U.S. so I can buy my Old Man bullets before the store closes.

Chapter III

A stabbing pain that starts at the soles of my feet and runs out my ears wakes me. It's dark, probably that "middle of the night" everyone talks about. The shadow standing over me in my bed is my Old Man. He gets off one more kick at the soles of my feet before I'm up and hitting the lights.

"I thought you'd never wake up, *háblate y háblate*," my Old Man says stepping off my bed. His voice comes out rushed like he's out of breath. His movements are jerky. He's high. "Where're the bullets I told you to buy?"

My feet hurt. I pull a brown paper sack from under the bed then knuckle the sleep out of my eyes to avoid making eye contact with him. "Your extra clips are loaded."

My Old Man stuffs boxes of .38 shells into a Samsonite overnight bag. He slides a leather sheath onto his belt. "Where're those clips?"

"I stuck 'em all in there." I point to the bank bag laying on my night stand. He takes the bag and pulls out two loaded clips and slides them into the leather sheath. My Old Man checks the four clips strapped to his left side and the .38 Super tucked in his waistband on the right side. He pulls the .38 a few times, practicing his quick draw, and then starts packing his shaving gear. I've seen my Old Man get ready for battle like this a lot.

My Old Man's .38 *escuadra* has only three serial numbers: 968. That means it was one of the first thousand .38 Supers that Colt made back in 1911. He had the gun refinished with the trigger, hammer, and barrel lock done in gold. The gold trimming stands out against the blue steel. It has gold and silver grips engraved with a rearing stallion. The stallion has diamonds for eyes and mane. It's a really cool fucking gun that only comes out for special occasions or for big fights.

"You're taking *la de tres cifras*?" I ask.

"*No es pa' menos*," my Old Man says. He stops packing and turns to me. "If I die in Veracruz, I want you to kill Roberto Alcocer. You know who I'm talking about?"

"The guy who picked us up at the airport in Veracruz that time we sent the Ford up," I say. "He drove us to *compadre* Nacho's house, the one with the peacocks." I picture Roberto Alcocer. I remember him thin but not skinny, a few inches taller than I am, with curly black hair and a real loose way of walking, like a drunk with a beat. We had a few beers together at a hotel in Veracruz when we were preparing another load of weed. He likes to laugh a lot and thinks I'm funny.

"*Ése*, him, you kill him if I don't make it back alive from Veracruz," my Old Man says. "He and his men have killed Felipe Lagunillas, and now they're trying to get my *compadre* Nacho."

"Why do they want to kill *compadre* Nacho?"

"Because my *compadre* is stepping up after Felipe—Nacho's next in line because he knows all of Felipe's contacts," my Old Man says holding out his thumb and pointer finger like a gun. "Nacho's killed six of Roberto's men. But Roberto has Nacho's *cuñado*, Juanito, hostage. Roberto even sent men to Felipe's funeral and shot up the coffin right there in front of the widow and everyone."

In the state of Veracruz, Felipe Lagunillas got a cut that he split with the governor on everything that was crooked—stolen cars, whores, numbers, cattle rustling, pot, *and* he got to name the state cops. While Felipe's cousin was governor, *Compadre* Nacho Zamora was chief of the state police and Felipe's right-hand man. Roberto Alcocer was Nacho's right-hand man and he was in charge of the municipal police for some town down there. But I guess people get tired of working for others all the time and Roberto saw his chance once he learned the ropes and stepped up; I can't really blame him. But he's showing no respect, shooting up coffins and shit, and I know Nacho's *cuñado*, Juanito. He took me and the rest of the kids to the beach once. As Roberto's hostage, Juanito's probably being tortured now, if he's alive at all.

"And you're going to Veracruz to help Nacho?" I say getting into my pants.

"What else can I do? My *compadre* Nacho helped me out that time Papá Cheto had the stroke. Don't you remember *esa carga* he gave me and never charged me a dime?"

Compadre Nacho was still chief of the state police in Veracruz when my grandfather suffered a stroke a couple years back. My Old Man needed money for doctors and shit. Nacho came through with fifty kilos of some pretty good pot he had busted—I think we sent that one up in a truck, but I can't remember right now. The pot didn't cost Nacho anything other than the beating he gave the guys he took it from.

"Why doesn't Nacho quit killing Roberto's men—just not fight with Roberto, so we can all get back to work?" I say without thinking.

My Old Man throws the T-shirts he was packing down on the bed. "*¿Qué chingados sabes tú? Te falta mucho pa' ser hombre.*"

"Who else is going with you to Veracruz?" I ask. "Maybe you should take me."

My Old man shakes his head—nice, like he appreciates the offer. "No one," he says. "I've sunk every cent I have into this trip to Nayarit. There's no money for *más gente*. I have to go alone, *a ver qué chingados.*" My Old Man grabs the overnight bag and the rest of his things and starts heading out. "You go and stay at my room at the El Camino and don't move from there until I call you. And remember, if I get killed, you get your ass to Veracruz and kill fucking Roberto Alcocer."

"What about school?"

"*Chingada madre mi'jo*, can't you think of anyone but yourself?" my Old Man says stomping his boots. "Go today and tell them you have to work for a week or two. Don't be off with that *pinche vieja*. And you better not be getting so fucked up that you don't hear the phone when I call."

He's gone before sunup.

I drop Raulito off at his school but before he gets out I say, "Don't worry about Dad going to Veracruz, everything's going to be cool."

"I know, he told me and Mom that we're going to the movies when he gets back," Raulito says. "Dad's bringing me back a ship in a bottle."

"A what?"

"One of those sailing ships stuffed in a bottle. The ones they sell on the beach."

"He's not going on vacation, dumb ass."

"He's just going to see his *compadres* like always. He'll bring it," Raulito says through the passenger side window. "Just watch."

I go to school and stay until lunch. After I finish my hamburger and chips, I score a dime bag then leave campus. I have my History and Government books and my English journal—fuck Science—in the back seat. I stop at the Easy Mart for a little jug of milk, Marlboros, and a pack of Zig-Zags then drive the eight miles to the bridge and into México. I nose my Mustang around the potholes—every pothole in the world has been gathered up and left in Reynosa—and through traffic to the Hotel El Camino across from the Volkswagen dealership. I get the key to my Old Man's room, #125, and tell Rafa behind the counter to put my milk in the fridge. In the room, I unload my books and folders onto one of the double beds. Then I crank up the AC and turn on the TV mounted on the wall and that's it, I'm moved in.

All I can get are Mexican channels, but it's okay because the old Mexican movies always have good-looking women. People make a big deal about American stars like Farrah and Wonder Woman or that dead chick, Marilyn Monroe. But fuck, if guys only knew about Mexican actresses there'd be more gringos learning Spanish. I don't care what anyone says: there has never been anyone prettier white or brown on any screen than Maria Felix or *las hermanas* Vásquez or with a better body than Tongolele, the dancing chick. I roll a joint on the nightstand fixed to the wall between the two double beds.

In México there's nothing lower than a *mariguano*.

Any time something really heinous happens, like a man chopping up his wife with a machete or some kid getting raped, the cops and newspapers will say *"porque andaba mariguano."* My Old Man says that when he was a kid, his mother used to lock him and his brothers and sisters in a back room with the drapes drawn shut whenever a known *mariguano* passed their house. He said my grandmother thought the whole family would break out in hives just for looking at a pothead. And that's pretty much how everyone in México feels about stoners. So I got to be careful when I smoke weed.

I gather up all the seeds and stems and flush 'em down the toilet. I flush five times to make sure nothing is left floating. I get my dime bag and wrap it around the pack of Zig-Zags and shove them up behind the sink. I open the bathroom window and stand in the shower and smoke the joint I rolled, putting the roach out on my tongue and stashing it behind the toilet for later. For cover, I light a Marlboro and let it burn in an ashtray. Now that I'm stoned, I lie down and start reading my Government book, but I put it down to whack off to this Mexican variety show that has a bunch of background dancers bouncing around in short shorts. I spend three days like this.

The first couple of days aren't so bad because I've got plenty to read. Rafa at the front desk brings me cereal in the morning then tacos at noon when he ends his shift. Rafa is married to my grandmother's sister's daughter, or some shit like that. On the third day, Rafa is off and I don't have a whole lot of money to tip the maids, so I have to budget the errands I send them on. I have four inch-long roaches and enough loose weed for about two joints. Even if Rafa is off again tomorrow, I can stretch the weed and survive on tortas and cokes for a day or two. After that something has to happen or else I won't have enough to pay the 75 cent toll on the bridge back to the U.S. Going home won't get me out of my jam because I'll only find Mom crawling the walls and ranting, "What are you doing home empty handed?" I need for my Old Man to call.

I take my mind off my money problems by thinking of ways to kill Roberto Alcocer. I don't own a gun, so I'll have to depend on my knife. It's a good knife, a Puma, with a stainless steel German blade about four fingers long. It cost my Old Man ninety bucks. My Old Man gave me the knife after some *comandante* gave him a better one. I haven't sharpened it in a while, but it has a good point and will still cut flesh if I press hard enough. I don't think it will break if I sink it into Roberto and hit a bone. I've never stabbed anyone with a knife. That's not what knives are for. Knives are for slashing motherfuckers. My Old Man always says that some fools are just not worth a fuck alive, but dead, these worthless fuckers turn into a problem that never goes away. So I never stab anyone. But I will slash someone's belly open if they try to put their hands on me.

I figure that a stab to the heart would mean having to go through ribs or those bones in the chest—I should've brought my fucking science book. My blade might not be long enough to reach any vital organs and only leave Roberto wounded. I'll have to slit Roberto's throat. That will kill him, but how am I going to get close enough to slit his throat, or even stab him for that matter, not to mention getting away? I'll have to catch him while he's taking a piss or when his back is turned or something. This seems cowardly, killing a man from behind. My Old Man would call him out into the street and shoot him down like Jacinto Treviño did the Texas Rangers in that *corrido*. I wish I had a gun.

It's already dark outside when Arturo shows up. I open the door and Arturo walks in and takes a big whiff and says, "*Huele a pura mota.*"

I open and close the door a few times to fan the room. Arturo pushes my books to one side and stretches out on one of the double beds. "Those books from your school, they're full of lies," he says. "Fucking *Estados Unidos* stole everything from México."

No sooner does he say this, he starts to snore. He smells like booze. I kick the side of the bed and say, "Hey you fat fuck, what'd you come for, to smell the room?"

Arturo stirs then sits up with a start. "Oh, I'm supposed to take you back to my house. Your dad's going to call."

I light a cigarette while Arturo splashes water on his face. "I've been drinking for two days," Arturo says. "What else is there to do while your dad is out of town?"

"We'll take my car," I say. Sober, Arturo drives like a fucking lunatic. Drunk, he rides sidewalks like a mail man who just got fired. I drive us up *Calle Río Mante* to Arturo's house. It's a big stucco two-story job with iron gates and a cinder-block fence. The top edge has shards of pointed glass cemented into the fence. The iron gates open to a drive way and a large cemented patio. One of Arturo's sisters, Chabela I think, is hosing down the patio. His nieces and nephews are running in and out of the house laughing and screaming. Another sister, Caro, is scrubbing laundry in an outside sink. There's a TV set up outside in the patio and Arturo's brother

Mario and some guys from the neighborhood are drinking beer and watching a soccer game.

I take a seat in front of the set while Arturo disappears inside. From the kitchen, I hear Arturo's mom yell, "My house isn't a public phone booth for *mafiosos.*"

"I built this house by working my ass off *en el otro lado,*" Arturo screams back. The guys sitting around the set begin to excuse themselves and head out of the patio leaving only me and Mario watching the game.

Mario puts his hand on my knee and says, "Don't pay any attention to Mama; she's just mad because Arturo's been drinking."

"I was concentrating on the game," I say and move my knee out of reach. Arturo motions me to come into the house and leads me to the living room. I take a seat next to the phone and try to play dumb while Arturo's mom whines about the phone bill. Arturo yells her down and turns to me and says, "She overcharges your dad for the phone bill every month."

My Old Man pays bills at a lot of houses, and I know they all gouge him. "I'm sure your mom's as honest as anyone," I say just as the phone rings and causes me to jump in my seat. Most guys don't realize just how much rides on a phone call. I get my ass chewed off all the time for not remembering that a guy can get locked up, lose a fortune, or even get killed just because some *pendejo* messed up a phone call—to this day I can't hear a phone ring without getting sweaty palms. I pick up. It's my Old Man.

"*¿Cómo te va*, Dad, you all right?" I say into the receiver.

"Things are still a little hot, but don't worry about it," my Old Man says on the other end. "Roberto put the new governor in his pocket before my *compadre* Nacho could. I'm going to be sending you some people over the next few days—almost all of the ex-governor's cabinet. They're going to call Arturo when they get to the bus station in Reynosa. Then Arturo's going to call you. You know what I'm talking about?"

"Yeah, sure."

"Take them to Chayo's. You got that?"

Chayo was nineteen when he started working for my Old Man. He grew up on the banks of the Río Bravo in Reynoso Díaz. My Old Man says that Chayo never loses a load because his mother used to wash out his baby bottle in the river. Chayo calls him *Apa* and my Old Man introduces Chayo to everyone as his *hijo de crianza*. I call Chayo *carnal*.

"You want me to tell *mi carnal* Chayo to take them swimming," I say.

"Tell Chayo I said I want these guys to spend turkey day with us."

"I take these guys to church?" I ask just to be sure I'm getting everything straight.

"Where else do we spend Thanksgiving, *pendejo*," my Old Man says. "I've got a few loose ends to tie up here. You do what I tell you and make sure everyone gets a chance to light a candle in front of *la Virgen*."

"So I don't have to stay at the hotel anymore?"

"How the fuck are you going to do what I told you from the hotel? *Chingada madre mi'jo*, I'm busy over here. I don't have time to explain every little detail for you. Use your fucking head."

I hate when I do stupid shit like that. The instructions are clear enough. Things got too hot for a bunch of the ex-governor's old cronies, so my Old Man is arranging safe passage out of Veracruz for them and I have to pick them up on this end in Reynosa. My Old Man has them call Arturo, so if they have a tail, it'll lead to Arturo before me. Arturo will get a description over the phone then pass it on to me. I'm to hang out at the bus station watching for guys who fit the bill until I'm sure it's them and nothing looks out of place. I make myself known, then drive up river with the guys to Reynosa Díaz where Chayo has a little farm. I leave the guys on the farm then drive back to Reynosa and over the bridge to the American side. After I cross over to the American side, I drive to La Joya and wait at Leo's Fast Mart. Chayo's usually eating tacos with the guys at the store by the time I get there. Then all I have to do is drive the guys back to our apartment in San Juan. Once on the American side, it doesn't matter if these guys know where we live. They might have been big deals in Veracruz but now they're fucking wetbacks; they're nobody in the U.S., and they have to depend on me for everything, so I can shake them down any way I see fit—hell, I'm the *patrón*.

On the way back to the hotel from Arturo's house, I notice some guys standing on street corners selling Mexican flags. Arturo explains that tomorrow is the 20th of November, the anniversary of the Mexican Revolution. I spend one last night at the hotel, smoking up my weed and listening to mariachis on the street from the balcony. By noon the next day, Arturo calls and says four guys, two in hats, one with a mustache, and one short fat fucker are waiting at the bus station. I gather my books and tip the maid a dollar to make sure the smoke smell is cleaned out of the room. I drive toward the bus station, but I'm stopped by a parade celebrating *el Aniversario de la Revolución*. I drive to Vicente el Loco's house to kill some time till the parade passes.

I spend about a half hour holding hands with Cynthia on Vicente's porch. She's wearing tight jeans and I can tell where two scoops of *nalgas* are poking out the bottom of her panties. I get hard. I tell her that I'm going to be busy for a while, that I have work. I promise to take her to Luby's Cafeteria in McAllen and a good movie as soon as the work lets up. She squeezes my hand and says, "*No te tardes.*"

I ask Cynthia to be my girlfriend, and she says yes. I try to give her a kiss, but she pushes my face away and says, "*Todavía no.*" Not yet is a whole lot different than 'not ever.' I hold her hand in mine and kiss it. I say goodbye and drive down to the bus station for the first of three loads of guys I have to smuggle into the U.S.

The first four guys say my Old Man personally escorted them to the bus station. They hadn't had time to pack anything but cash. I spend the next few days running around town getting these guys soap and shampoo, cigarettes, food, shit like that, and for everything they give me fifties and hundred dollar bills and always tell me to keep the change.

The short fucker is Gastón de la Cuerda. He was *Jefe de Transito* for the state of Veracruz before the governor's departure from office. Now, he's a fugitive. Gastón brought his boy Friday, an ugly motherfucker we all call *Pico Chulo*. The two guys in hats are this rich kid and his secretary. As far as I can tell, the rich kid has a construction company that got a lot of state contracts kicked its way, schools, hospitals, probably even an orphanage that never got built. What do I care, he has cash. I make over a thousand bucks running errands for these fools the next couple of weeks.

My mom helps me rent the house next door to *el primo* Bocho's on Ebony street and sets me and the guys up with a table and a couple of beds she gets secondhand. I make another trip to the bus station in Reynosa. I pick up Juanito, *Compadre* Nacho's brother-in-law, who just recently got released from being kidnapped. The skin around his eyes and nose is rubbed raw like a red glossy Lone Ranger's mask from being blindfolded for ten days. Juanito's wrists are cut deep all around and he walks like he'll drop a nut if he takes a full step. Juanito's scared he's ruined for life because while they had him hostage Roberto's men put the *chicharra*, an electric prod, to his balls.

I take Juanito back to the El Camino and hustle up a couple of whores—I can't take whores to my Old Man's room or the maids will tell Mom. Earlier, Rafa rented a room to a young couple who only used it for a few hours, so he's able to get it for the rest of the night for free. The whores show up and luckily one is a nurse and she's able to patch up Juanito before she gets him off. The one I get is a pretty whore with big tits. She's so pretty I want to kiss her on the mouth, but no whore ever kisses on the mouth no matter how much extra you offer to pay.

That morning, my Old Man tracks me to the hotel and tells me to pick up *compadre* Nacho and his *pistolero*, el Cachoon, at the bus station. By that evening I have seven guys—all the ex-governor's men—holed up at the house in San Juan.

I'm scoring coke for *compadre* Nacho, just about every gram in the colonia, which gets me a lot of respect in the neighborhood. *Compadre* Nacho tips better than Gastón and all the rest of the guys put together. He's even giving me cash to give to my mom, his *comadre*, for a Thanksgiving dinner that I didn't get to go to. Also money for bills, rent, and anything else she needs while my Old Man's out. Everything is cool on my end, but my Old Man still hasn't made it back. He checks in everyday, mostly just to bitch me out because "it doesn't take a fortune teller to know what I did at the hotel all this time." No, it doesn't take a fortune teller; Arturo or Rafa or any of the maids at the hotel will do. And every time I ask him when he'll be home, all my Old Man says is, "Don't worry 'bout the mule, just pull the wagon."

Chayo shows up at the little house on Ebony and calls me into his truck. He reaches his long arm—Chayo is built like a Tarzán Mexicano—under the seat and pulls out a brown paper bag and lays it on the seat between us.

"*Apa* said for you to stash this somewhere only you know," Chayo says. "There's a kilo of soda in that bag. Don't go getting all fucked up on it, *Carnalito*."

"No shit," I say palming the bag testing for weight. "This is a kilo of cocaine, a million bucks like they say on TV."

We laugh. Anyone who has ever moved drugs lives in search of that street where the DEA says a kilo is worth a million bucks; it's like trying to find El Dorado. Chayo says, "*Apa* is sending up seventy more."

"Whose are they?"

"They were Felipe's," Chayo says. "Be careful with this shit. Dad sent it up separate for a reason."

"Any word on when my Old Man is coming home?"

"*Mañana*," Chayo says. *Mañana* is Mexican for whenever it happens.

I take the bag and stash it in the trunk of my car then park my car behind the house and pop the hood. I keep tight-lipped about it other than to say that the car is fucked up and we'll have to walk to the corner store for beer. I watch that car nonstop for two nights. On the second night I do a line of coke with *compadre* Nacho, just to keep awake. I use my license to fix me a rail on a plate and like a dumb ass I leave it and a rolled up bill lying on the only table in the fucking house.

The coke helps me stay awake most of the night, but by sunup, I'm overcome with sleep. A hand slaps down on my chest and through a glare of sunlight I make out my Old Man standing over me. My license and the bill are on my chest. I sit up and my Old Man slaps me across the head with a rolled up newspaper. I move in time to catch the newspaper before it hits me a second time. I open it and read the head line: *Record decomiso de cocaína en Saltillo.*

"Nothing had better have happened to that bag Chayo gave you while you were getting fucked up with these fools," my Old Man says.

"I've been watching it for two days now," I say pointing through the open window to my Mustang parked in the back yard.

"Don't move it until I get rid of these guys."

"And all that other coke fell, seventy kilos?" I say pointing to the headline in the newspaper.

"These guys aren't too lucky. They're like el Chapparo. They couldn't get a load up to the border even with a presidential escort."

"What happened to el Chaparro?"

"He went and wrecked our car," my Old Man says.

"Oh, no. Our load of weed got lost too? Ah, hell, now what are we going to do?" Two loads lost and not a cent to our names to reinvest. It's like the fucking stock market is crashing down around me.

"I've got my name don't I?" my Old Man says. "When one door closes, another opens." My Old Man points to my Mustang sitting in the back yard. "Call Pepe, *el hijo de* Navarro, and tell him we have work. Then get me some coffee."

I start putting on my shoes—I never take

anything off but my shoes to sleep whenever I'm around a lot of guys. My Old Man notices the bulge in my pants and asks, "What's that?" I pull out the wad of cash I had raked together from doing errands for Gastón and *compadre* Nacho and say, "Tips."

"Good," my Old Man says and takes the wad and peels off a twenty for me.

I ask my Old Man before he leaves my room, "What about Roberto Alcocer and that stuff going on in Veracruz?"

"Oh, that," my Old Man says. "*Yo tengo mi nombre*. People hear my name and they have to respect it. These guys can go back home. Roberto won't touch them as long as they stay out of his way. Besides, they have to worry about the *Federal de Caminos* in Saltillo tracing that car in the newspaper back to Gastón and my *compadre* Nacho. But that's their problem. I've done more than anyone else would've."

"So I don't have to do anything to Roberto Alcocer?"

"Like you could do anything," my Old Man says. "Don't worry 'bout the mule, just pull the wagon, *mi'jo*."

I get my Old Man's keys and take his car to the corner store and place a call to Pepe Cantú. Pepe is the son of the man who helped my grandfather and father fix their residency papers back in '56. Navarro Cantú was a pretty big man around field workers who needed their papers fixed. But Pepe grew up to be an *arponero*, a harpooner, a guy who shoots up heroin, and spends most of his time in jail for possession. On the inside, he made a lot of contacts with guys who buy dope. We only call Pepe when we have hard drugs to sell—heroin, coke, 'ludes. For our regular line of work, pot, we have a shitload of guys who call us. Pepe says he'll be over as soon as he can get his morning fix. I buy my Old Man his coffee and start back to the house. As I'm backing up, I notice a bag in the back seat. In the bag there's a felt jewelry box and a ship in a bottle.

Chapter IV

We got thirty-five thousand dollars for the kilo of cocaine. It was barely enough money to carry us through Christmas and into spring. The state police in Nayarit found papers with el Chaparro's name on them in the car along with our load of 150 kilos of *cola de borrego*. My Old Man lays down an extra grand for the chief of police in Nayarit to report finding the car free of documents. I don't know how much he paid to get half the load back. I know we took a loss because we've already paid the federal police to let the whole 150 kilos go through all the checkpoints from Nayarit to Reynosa. The money from that load barely covers expenses and first and last month's rent for my mom's new brick house off of FM 495 on San Juan's north side. My Old Man and I still have one of the apartments across from the Shrine that we keep as our office.

It's March, but the days are already getting hot, even though the devastating freeze of 1983 hit just weeks earlier. They're still cleaning up the ruined orchards, houses with busted pipes, and split engines. We've got work too.

I'm serving drinks to Armando and Abel Culardo while they do a deal with Chicho Calvo in our apartment. The Culardos have a few hundred pounds of weed, and Chicho has the client. Chicho was big-time back in the '70s when he had the Texas State Troopers in his pocket and could land Cessnas full of weed north of the checkpoint on Highway 281. The troopers didn't give a fuck. They would block the road with their black and whites, glaring their Ray Bans at anyone who asked why, while we unloaded and refueled. I always wondered what the other drivers thought when they saw a plane taking off right on the highway. Chicho had to stop flying in loads after his contacts with the State Troopers got promoted to desk jobs. It's hard times now, and Chicho is scuffling around like the rest of us, making due on small hook-ups till something bigger comes along.

Chicho, or anyone else who sells dope, will never allow the client and the dealer to meet. If the supplier ever meets the money man, "*el bueno*," then the middle man, "*la conecta*," is out of work in a hurry. The Culardos brought Chicho samples of the weed they have for sale in two quart-sized ziplock bags. Chicho takes the *muestra* to his client to see if he likes the weed and gives him his price. He comes back to our apartment with the cash and tells the Culardos that his guy likes the *lima-lemón*, but not the red-bud.

Because of the freeze and everyone being out of work, weed is doing good and a *conecta* can make anywhere from fifty to a hundred bucks a pound for playing middle man on a deal. This is when the price of marijuana is up, but when it's cutting season and there's a lot of weed around, you're lucky to make twenty-five bucks a pound for connecting a buyer to the seller. Chicho says his guy will take a hundred pounds of the lime-colored weed. Abel leaves in Chicho's car to weigh and load the weed while Armando stays behind to handle the money. Armando sells to Chicho at $250 a pound and Chicho turns around and sells to his client for $350 a pound. Chicho and Armando go into my room to count out thirty-five thousand dollars on one of the twin beds.

When they come out, Chicho hands me a wad of twenties and says, "Here's your dad's quarter. I still have to give another quarter to my brother Elmo for introducing me to his gringo, so tell your dad I only made fifty cents myself."

Armando hands me a hundred dollar bill and says, "That's for you. Tell your dad I'll give him his cut from my end when I see him in Reynosa."

Abel shows up with Chicho's now loaded car and everyone takes off. I stash the twenty-five hundred dollars Chicho gave me in one of my Old Man's coats hanging in the closet and then I clean up the glasses and ash trays. My Old Man shows up minutes later with his new "*secretario*," Alberto Prietón, and some groceries.

My Old Man always says, "when one door closes another opens up," and he's right. That's what I used to like about working *en la movida*, the way things fall together. If my Old Man hadn't cut that kilo of coke from the rest of that load coming out of Veracruz, we wouldn't have had any money to buy half of our weed back from the police in Nayarit. If we hadn't lost half of that load, we wouldn't have gone to Tampico to sell el Gordo Sótano some guns. And if we hadn't gone to Tampico, we would've never met Alberto Prietón.

Alberto, or Beto, is from Tampico. He's a tall, thin, dandified, dark, almost black man in his early forties who wears polyester pants that have no belt loops. He studied in a seminary with Jesuit priests and knows about medicine and can prescribe shit for whatever ails you. He says he's written for newspapers and calls himself a *periodista* and I believe him because he's a busybody motherfucker— there ain't shit you can say about anything that Beto won't have a comment for.

We got Beto out of the trunk of a car. We— my Old Man, Chaparro, and me—were in Tampico selling some guns and ammunition to el Gordo

Sótano a week after el Chaparro lost that load in Nayarit. Sótano was about to send his men to give Beto *piso*, to floor him, when my Old Man spoke up and made Sótano get Beto out. Beto was yelling from the trunk how it is "illogical" to kill him because he is too much of an "asset." He goes on about how he contributes to the group and how keeping him alive is sound business sense. I've seen more than a few guys beg for their lives, but Beto is the funniest. My Old Man must think so too because he saves Beto and makes him his *secretario personal.*

I tell my Old Man that Chicho and the Culardos flipped a hundred pounds from our apartment a few minutes ago and that his cash from Chicho's end is in his coat in the closet. Beto's helping me put up the groceries when my Old Man runs into the kitchen holding a ziplock bag full of weed.

"¿*Qué chingados es esto*?" my Old Man says.

I look into the ziplock bag and say, "That's *mota*, Dad."

"I know it's fucking *mota*. What's this fucking weed doing here?"

"Looks like that red bud Chicho's client didn't like. I guess Armando left it here after they did their deal."

"Or you got it and stashed it in the box where we put the dirty clothes thinking I wouldn't find it," my Old Man says.

"I thought they took everything with them when they left," I say as my Old Man squares off in front of me.

Beto moves in between me and my Old Man and says in that dandified way of talking he has, "I don't see how el Johnny could know anything about this marijuana other than what he just told you, Don Julio. Chicho and the Culardos had just left when we arrived, so Johnny would've had very little time to hide this bag and still be out here cleaning up when we walked through the door."

Beto turns to me and asks, "Where was Chicho when the business was being conducted?"

"Right there in the living room most of the time, except when they went into the room to count the money," I say.

"There you have it, Don Julio," Beto says to my Dad. "These gentlemen must've left that bag in your room after they settled accounts."

My Old Man looks at me and says, "Yeah, that might be, but you don't know this kid yet. He's a *pinche mariguano.*"

"Your son," Beto says taking the bag of weed out of my Old Man's hand, "did not act like he was doing anything suspicious or out of the ordinary when we arrived and immediately directed you to the gains of the day where he had secured them. He may be many things, but he is not foolish enough to send you into the same room looking for money where he has just hidden something he doesn't want you to find."

"You can always ask Armando," I say. "He said he would see you in Reynosa to give you your cut from his end."

"Is this all the money they gave you?" my Old Man says taking the wad of twenties out of his pocket.

"Yeah, and a hundred he tipped me," I say, showing him the bill. "I was planning on using thirty-five bucks to pay for this test some kids are taking in Harlingen. You know, for school."

My Old Man snatches the hundred from my hand then throws me two twenties. "Use that for your test," he says then goes back into our room. I pick up the twenties and turn around to find Beto holding the ziplock bag open.

"Here Johnny," Beto says. "Take a pinch out of this bag, you've earned it."

I reach into the bag then pull my hand out with out grabbing anything. "How do I know you're not just setting me up to put the finger on me with my Old Man later?"

"You don't," Beto says shaking the bag and filling the kitchen with the smell of fresh weed.

I reach into the bag and grab a handful of weed and wrap it in a paper towel I stuff in my pocket. "You'll be in just as much trouble as me if my Old Man finds out about this," I say.

"I know," Beto says. "We'll just have to learn to trust each other."

"Fuck that trust bullshit. You might be his right hand now, but I'm his son. He might kick my ass, but he'll definitely kill you. Remember, we got you out of a trunk, so you kinda owe me your life. If those guys hadn't listened to my Old Man and let you go, we would've had to pull iron on them."

"Are you referring to that little misunderstanding in Tampico when we first met?" Beto asks while he wraps up the weed in cellophane. "Sótano and his men wouldn't have done anything to me. I'm too valuable. I can make people money."

"Guys like my Old Man and Sótano care more about people respecting them than they do about money. You must've done something or they wouldn't have had you in the trunk of a car."

"There were a few members of our group who were envious of the connections I was making," Beto says like it's no big deal.

"Shit, envy, that's more than enough to get a guy killed." I can't get a make on Beto. He's not stupid, but he says a lot of ignorant shit. Most guys who work for my Old Man just do what they're told, but Beto makes suggestions and is always throwing his two cents into everything. He's been cool with me, so I give him a bit of advice. "My Old Man isn't envious of anyone, but if you ever play him for a *pendejo*, you're going to wish we never got you out of that trunk in Tampico."

"You're smart for a man your age," Beto says. "What's this about a test you're going to take?"

I figure Beto's only trying to change the subject but I go along because the truth is I really don't have anyone else to talk this over with. El Chaparro's been laying low since he almost got busted in Nayarit, and no one else in my family has ever been to college, but Beto studied with those priests and might be able to give me a heads up.

"There's this big test kids have to take if they want to go to college."

"You mean an entrance exam," Beto says. "What college do you plan on attending?"

"Oh, no, I don't plan on going to college. I just want to see if I can pass the test."

"Why aren't you going to enroll?"

"There's no money for that kind of thing," I say. "I just want to see if I can pass. Then I'll find some work. My oldest brother manages a restaurant in Dallas. I might go to work with him, or I can do cowboy work with my other brother Junior. Or I can do roofing with my brother Rubén in Houston. I haven't decided who I want to work for yet." I seriously doubt any of my brothers would give me work, much less a place to stay.

Beto gives me the "you're full of shit" smile and says, "That's a good plan, but while you're deciding which of those fine jobs to take, why don't you get a formal education?" Beto puts his hand on my shoulder. "Johnny, your father and I are on the brink of doing some pretty big things. When the time comes for you to go to college, I will talk to your father for you and make sure he sees how important it is."

"We'll see," I say knocking away Beto's hand. I go into the bathroom and roll a joint to smoke before school in the morning. So my dad and Beto are up to "big things." Beto is new and doesn't know that we're always up to "big things." What's my Old Man got now? A new connection for scoring weed? A buyer? Maybe we hit the lottery and some *compadre* just got named *comandante*. Whatever it is, I'll have to carry a message, wait for a phone call, or deliver a bag of money sooner or later, so I'll figure it out. Beto and my Old Man aren't as smart as they think they are, or I'm not as dumb as they think I am. I haven't gotten around to figuring which is which.

The next day at school, I go into the counselor's office to get information on the ACT. After the white secretary sends me to a rack loaded with pamphlets for trucking and vocational schools, I tell her I need a signature to take an advanced welding class, and she lets me in to see the counselor. The counselor is disappointed I don't want to pursue welding. I hit him up for the location and registration forms and he stares at me with his hands folded on his desk in front of him and says, "It costs thirty-five dollars, you know."

I flash the counselor the two twenties my Old Man gave me and he hands me a form. I have to take the form and a money order to Harlingen High School two Saturdays before graduation and sit for the test.

School goes by like a stroll through the Sahara. It's hot. Just getting to class between buildings leaves you with beads of sweat rolling down your crack. Most of the kids are either talking about where they're going to college or which state they're going to work the fields in. There's a college in Edinburg the kids call Taco Tech that I can get into and still be able to live at home. Or I can go with my *tío* Bocho to Iowa and work on a pea farm.

At home my mom is all pissed off because my sister's boyfriend has been slapping her around. It's as if my sister believes that if she fucks enough white guys, she'll eventually turn white herself.

"I don't know why God wasted balls on men," Mom says. "If I was a man, I would've already taken care of that white trash when my daughter first started running around with him."

"You're the one who used to cover for Lourdes so she could go out with this guy," I say.

"Shut up," my Mom says. "You have less balls than anybody. You can do something to help your sister, but you just turn your back on her. I can't believe you turned out to be so horrible."

"What the hell you want me to do? Give me some gas money and I'll drive up to Houston and take a bat to that gringo piece of shit."

"Don't be stupid," Mom says handing me the phone. "All you have to do is call my *compadre* Alex and tell him to send someone over to beat the shit out of this punk who's hurting *mi'ja*."

"Alex is your *compadre*, why don't you make the call?" *Compadre* Alex has been indicted for murder three times. The last guy he killed was a cop in a Houston night club. The cop walks up to Alex and puts a .357 magnum to his head and says, "You're Alex Caballero."

Alex says, "I am."

The cop says, "*Te crees muy chingón.*"

Alex says, "No, but I won't take shit from you." Then Alex gets up pulling his knife and slits the cop's throat. Alex hired Percy Foreman to get him acquitted for self defense because the cop never identified himself. Foreman has a picture of *compadre* Alex hanging in his office.

"So your dad can think I'm fucking him," Mom says. "I can't believe you're such a *poco hombre.*"

Just like that my Mom calls me a pussy and I'm on the phone with three-times-indicted-for-murder-and-always-acquitted *compadre* Alex. This is the only guy my Old Man acknowledges as a fellow man of balls.

"My sister is having a hard time with her man," I say sharing the phone with my mom so she can hear the conversation. "It's really upsetting my Mom."

"Well, we can't have that," *compadre* Alex says over the phone. "Family is the most sacred thing a man can have."

"Mom's scared Dad will get real mad if he finds out," I say.

"No, we can't have my *compadre* flying off the handle and getting in trouble over something so simple," *compadre* Alex says. "Someone else should talk to this boy and ask him to behave."

My mom tugs on my sleeve and whispers, "Tell him not to," and then she runs her finger across her throat. "He still has to pay child support for those two babies."

"We think the same way you do," I say into the phone. "I'm sure just a good talking to is all he needs to understand how things are."

"Does this young man still live in that house where my boys laid the carpet that one time?"

My mom nods her head yes and I say, "Yeah, the same place."

"Tell my *comadre* not to worry about a thing," *compadre* Alex says. "I'm sure some friend will see that this boy is doing wrong and talk to him about it by this weekend. Say hello to my *compadre* for me."
"You see," Mom says after I hang up. "That wasn't so hard. *Pinches hombres* always make a big deal about nothing."

The night before the test, my sister calls and I just happen to answer the phone.
"Johnny, you son of a bitch, Mom told me what you did," Lourdes shouts over the phone.
"What the hell are you talking about," I say.
"They broke Steve's jaw, you motherfucker," Lourdes says hanging on the last part to where it sounds like "fuck-errrrr" like she's a redneck or something.
"I still don't know what you're talking about."
"You watch, you little motherfucker, I'm going to call the police and tell 'em it was you. You're going to get fucked in jail, Johnny. Just wait and see."

She hangs up before I can remind her that this is the same guy who has been knocking her around. I get my supplies ready for tomorrow's test and head back to the apartment.

My Old Man is waiting by the door as I come in. He grabs me and throws me on the couch. I fall sitting and barely manage to roll to the floor to duck a blow my Old Man swings at me. I get back on my feet and put some distance between us and see that he has his gun in his hand. I notice that we're not alone. Julio Dávalos is sitting on the couch I just bounced off of and Beto is standing by the kitchen. The unmistakable click of a safety being dropped fills the room. I feel the front of my pants grow warm then cold as my boots fill with piss. I take a soggy step closer to Dávalos, and he bounces off the couch and into the kitchen.

"What'd I do?" I ask looking for something to hide behind.

"*No te hagas pendejo*," my Old Man says jabbing at the air in front of him with his gun. "Your mother told me you made that call to my *compadre* Alex."

"She told me to call him."

"And suddenly, you become obedient," my Old Man says—the gun now leveled and steady, very steady. "Your whore sister is saying she's going to call the law. *Pendejo*, you know what kind of shit you'll put me through if my *compadre* Alex gets into trouble over this? If anything happens between me and my *compadre*, you're going to pay. Now get the fuck out of my sight."

I go to the bedroom too afraid to clean up and peel off my clothes and try to go to sleep but I'm still awake when the birds start to chirp outside the window in the morning. I shower and get dressed before anyone else is up. I'm almost out the door when my Old Man's voice stops me in my tracks.

"What time you going to be home?"

"Just as soon as I finish this test," I say, hoping he still remembers he said it was okay.

"You meet me at La Majada when you get back from Harlingen. We've got work," he says then goes back to bed.

I point my Mustang to the rising sun and set out on new highway 83. The morning is spectacular. I've heard guys in the movies say that about mornings, spectacular, and I think this is one of those. The wasteland the freeze made of the Valley is starting to come back to life in millions of blossoms forming a rich green fuzz over the ground. The freshly tilled earth smells moist and the hands in the fields trudge over the broken ground smiling, happy for the work.

I'm going to take a test that if I pass, I can go to college. Beto said he'd talk to my Old Man for me. My Old Man said we had work just before I left so maybe we can manage to pay for a semester or two. I look out my window at the fields rolling by and I lean on my horn.

"Hey, *primos*, I'm going to college," I yell over the rushing wind. Some guys from the fields wave to me as I speed past the lumbering trucks, honking my horn and yelling like a loon.

I get to Harlingen High and find the testing location with no problem. There's about a hundred and fifty kids lined up around the cafeteria, mostly white, but at least a quarter of us are *raza*. They get our money and seat us apart from each other at long tables in the cafeteria. This little old silver-haired white lady whose face could be on a frozen pie box is handing out the test booklets. I get a seat between a white pimple-faced boy and this cute Mexican chick with dark eyes and long hair tied into a big loop behind her head. The white kid is picking his nose. The cute chick is making the sign of the cross over and over while belting out Hail Marys under her breath.

Old miss pie box gets to the white kid and hands him his test and says, "Good luck, sweetie," just like she said to the white kid before him.

But when the old lady gets to me, she just drops the test and shuffles on. Before she gets to the girl next to me I say, "What, no good luck sweetie for me?"

The old lady turns around and says, "All you Mexicans are just wasting our time. Everyone knows you're just here for the financial aid."

I jump out of my seat and say, "Hey, you can't. . . ."

This guy in a short-sleeved shirt and tie comes barreling over to me and says, "You have a problem, mister?"

"She just said Mexicans. . . ."

The guy snatches my test booklet from off the table and says, "Would you like to turn in your test?"

"No, it's just that she said. . ."

"Then I suggest you sit down and quit interrupting," he says holding the test away from me like he was afraid I would try to snatch it out of his hand.

I look around and the white kid has his finger up his nose and is snickering away at me. The cute chick is praying and making the sign of the cross faster than ever. Everyone in that room knows what I'm going to do even before I do. I can feel the heated stares of every brown eye in that cafeteria. They look at me like *I'm* embarrassing *them*. All the white kids sit with little half smiles waiting for what they know will happen next.

I sit down. The guy in the short-sleeved shirt and tie lets my test booklet fall to the table. I scoop up the test booklet and hug it to my chest. The guy in the short-sleeved shirt and tie stands over me for the entire test. And I just sit there with my head bowed, taking my test, knowing that life's going to be that much harder from now on.

Chapter V

There isn't much traffic going into Reynosa. Not as much as there is going out, anyway. I inch my Mustang over the international bridge, checking out the people stuck in line waiting to cross into the U.S. I'm still pissed over frozen pie box lady and the short-sleeved guy. There's a melon-faced man driving a Dodge. His windows are down and the car is overheating. His wife, a dark woman with sweat running down the sides of her face, is using a piece of newspaper to fan two kids sitting in the back seat. The melon-faced man is sticking his head out the window watching the steam flow from under the hood of the Dodge. I pull up next to him and say, "*¿A qué chingados vas al otro lado?*"

The melon-faced man tears himself away from the steaming hood and says, "I have to buy milk and diapers."

"You've got no business going to the other side."

"I have to buy milk and diapers," he says.

I cross the bridge and pull up to *la línea* and shake hands with the *aduanal* on duty. The Mexican customs official whistles to his partners and I'm waved through the inspection area. I pull into the parking lot of La Majada, but I wait a while before getting out of the car. My knuckles are jetting up boney white from the steering wheel. I wring my hands around the wheel wishing it was the neck of that guy in short sleeves and tie. I pound the wheel with the palm of my hand. That's for the silver-haired lady. I get out of the car and throw a kick at the rear tire and the hub cap pries off and hits the pavement with a clatter loud enough to make the parking lot attendant look up from his newspaper. I tell him to see to the hub cap and he hops right to it.

There's the crippled midget sitting under the large window that looks into the pit where goats are roasting on spits in front of La Majada. He holds his little hand up to me and I kick the plaid shopping bag full of coins lying next to him and say, "I'm not your *pendejo, enano.*"

The midget looks up and smiles, "Oh, sorry Johnny. I didn't notice it was you."

"You were too busy making with the lamb eyes."

The midget laughs. "A man's got to work."

"You've got the best job in México."

"*No me quejo,*" the midget says.

"No, no sense in complaining," I say and go into the restaurant.

My Old Man, el Chaparro, Beto, and Onésimo are sitting at a corner table—we always sit at corner tables. I order a beer on my way to them and the waiter clicks his heels and scurries behind two swinging doors to fetch me a Corona. My Old Man has a half-empty shot glass of tequila and a plate of cut limes in front of him.

"So I'm sitting in front of Roberto Alcocer at this restaurant in Veracruz just like we are right here, *vez*?" my Old Man says. "Roberto says, 'What are you doing here Julio,' and I say 'I've come to put an end to these *chingaderas* so we can all get back to work.' 'Did you bring gente, Julio?' Roberto says. I look Roberto straight in the eyes and say, '*Bastantes*, I brought enough men to turn Veracruz into rubble.'" My Old Man slams his palm down on the table and tequila splashes out of his glass. "And just like that, Roberto releases Juanito and the other hostages and the fighting ends in Veracruz. I have a name and people know that when I say something, I mean it." My Old Man does the rest of his shot and snaps his fingers for another. "I should've let them keep fighting. After losing that load, Veracruz closed down for us anyway."

"*Record Decomiso*," I say, quoting from the article that covered our lost load of coke.

"We should've used our own drivers to carry that load," el Chaparro says.

My Old Man shakes his head. "You were busy losing our load of *mota*. I'm glad you weren't driving up that coke from Veracruz. I'd be stuck with the bill if you were behind the wheel. Anyone can lose a load of weed and bounce back, but coke? *No'mbre qué chingados.*"

El Chaparro reaches into his back pocket and pulls out a folded piece of newspaper. He unfolds the paper to a picture of a car with the trunk all smashed up. Under the picture the caption reads: *Victim of traffic accident loaded with marijuana.* El Chapparo folds up the paper and says, "Mine wasn't a *chingazo de soda*, but *mota* keeps reporters busy just the same."

My Old Man turns to me and asks, "*¿Como te fue en el otro lado?*"

"The test didn't seem that hard, but I hate being around gringos," I say. "I don't want to go to college anyway."

"Somebody give you shit?" my Old Man asks. "What do you expect? You smell like *mota* all the time."

"I didn't do anything. The gringos giving the test treated me like a *mojado*," I say and drain the rest of my beer.

"Fuck 'em," my Old Man says and orders me a shot of tequila.

"I don't know why you don't go to college here in México, Johnny," Beto says.

"You could study law right here in Reynosa," Onésimo says. "I know all the *maestros* who teach law at El Bravo University. I guarantee you'll never fail a test or be counted absent."

"No, no, no," Beto says. "He needs to study in a much more prestigious university, like the *Autónoma de Nuevo León* or at the *Tech de Monterrey*."

"I can't go to those schools," I say salting down my wrist so I can take my shot of tequila. There's no fucking way on earth I'm going to say my Old Man can't afford to send me to college in front of anybody and expect to keep a tooth in my mouth. "You have to be a Mexican to study in México."

"And what do you think you are?" my Old Man asks. "If a cat goes into an oven, she doesn't have biscuits. She has *gatitos*. It's the same thing when a Mexican crosses some line a gringo drew and has a family. His kids are still Mexican no matter how far north they're born."

"If that's a worry for you, I can get you a birth certificate that says you're a Mexican, Johnny," el Chapparro says.

"We can use the *Sindicato de Aduanas* to pull some strings and get him into the state university in Monterrey," Beto says.

"There you go," my Old Man says. "We'll stop by Monterrey on our way back from Durango. Chapparro, you get to work on that birth certificate before we leave. I want a good job, no photocopy bullshit. *Todo chalán-balán* so *mi'jo* doesn't have any trouble farther down the line."

"Don't worry," el Chapparro says. "I got a *compadre* who works at the Civil Registry in Río Bravo."

"And that's it?" I ask. "I won't have to be a gringo anymore?"

"You'll be a *mojado*, but in reverse," el Chapparro says.

Everyone laughs, but I don't mind. In the U.S., I'm a beaner, wetback, greaser, a minority. But in México, I'm Don Julio Cortina's son, a guy who gets shit done for him by just needing it to be done. I'm going to study law. I'm going to be a fucking *Licenciado*. I'm going to have a license to rob motherfuckers and that's better than a get out of jail free card. I'm going to be the get out of jail card only I'm sure as fuck not going to be free. I'm so happy I forget to ask why we're going to Durango.

El Chaparro, Beto, my Old Man, my big brother Junior and me are crammed into a '79 Dodge Magnum, and we're hauling ass down a slim strip of asphalt barely wide enough for two big rigs to pass each other head on. This is *la Carretera Panamá*, or the Panama Highway. With a name like that, I always pictured it to be something more than the rut-lined potholed ribbon of what must be one of the most dangerous roads in the world. My Old Man is driving and he is pleased at how fast our car is and floors it down the straightaways and fishtails the curves.

We pass through Monterrey and climb the sierra toward Saltillo, but before we get there we turn right in Ramos Arispe and head to Torreón, Coahuila. In a town called Paila, we stop at the only visible business, a restaurant called Lourdes-28 de Agosto, because that is my sister's name and birth date and my Old Man says a coincidence like this will bring us luck on our trip. We get coffee and beefsteak rancheros plus a couple of six packs for the road and tear off at breakneck speed through mountain passes overlooking ridges that don't seem to have a bottom. My Old Man announces that in a matter of hours we've crossed terrain that took Pancho Villa thirteen days to cover. This pleases my Old Man.

Coming down from the sierra, the landscape changes with each bend in the road. One minute we're rolling past adobe huts surrounded by organ cactus fences only to hit the next town and find stucco-finished houses sitting behind manicured lawns. Some towns are little more than a string of houses marked by a rusted highway marker, while others have curbs and traffic lights and whistle-happy transit cops who try to shake us down because we're traveling with out-of-state plates. We all laugh at the transit cops when my Old Man gets off with his .38 sticking out of his waistband, flashing his badge that says he's a *comandante*. They see the *charola*, make with the "*perdón jefe*," and open traffic for us all the way out of town.

In between the towns are wide-open areas of rolling brush and gorged earth. Rocky mesas lie in the distance, and all kinds of cactus guard both sides of the road from the paddle leaf nopal to organ cactus, barrel cactus, and flowering Joshua trees. It's like God made a beautiful garden of things, all with thorns.

From Paila we hit Torreón and we travel over a long-ass bridge into the state of Durango. We go through Gomez Palacio and then turn left. We pass through the town of Cuencamé, Durango where my grandfather and Facundo Ramos—the father of the guy we stole those sheep from—had a slaughterhouse. My Old Man says they closed the slaughterhouse when a horse kneeled for mercy before getting a sledgehammer between the eyes. When we reach the town of Francisco I. Madero, a road sign informs us that Durango, Durango is only fifty-five kilometers away. Even with the stop in Paila and fooling around with the transit cops along the way, we're able to make the trip from Reynosa through four states to Durango, Durango in less than nine hours.

We cross downtown Durango, and it's nice like any other city I've been in, big buildings, and a lot of people walking around in suits and uniforms mingled with scruffy-looking bums and street merchants. There's a statue of Pancho Villa by a rotunda we take that puts us on the road out of town. Traffic begins to die down to a few brightly painted buses bellowing black smoke with every gear shift and produce trucks that have to slow down to go around guys riding in horse-drawn carts. My Old Man says this is where John Wayne filmed over twenty movies, and I believe it because every store, restaurant, telephone *casseta* we stop at has a picture of the Duke hanging next to pictures of Pancho Villa.

At one of these *cassetas,* my Old Man makes a phone call and a half hour later a Suburban double parks next to our car. Four guys with AK-47's get off the Suburban and take turns shaking hands with my Old Man. My Old Man makes with the introductions and one of the guys, el Güero Gil, gets in the car with my Old Man, Beto, and el Chaparro. My brother Junior and I ride in the Suburban following behind my father's car. El Chano, the driver, points out all the spots where they've had shootouts with the military—only he calls shootouts "*hechando candela.*" And I tell about how my Old Man "*arregló una bronca*" in Veracruz.

We go on exchanging war stories for about an hour until we get to a gate with an arched sign over it that reads: *El Bisonte.* The gate is manned by two guys, one carrying an AK-47and another guy toting a Colt AR-15. The guy with the AR-15 opens the gate for us and we drive through it down a paved road between fields of shoulder-high corn to the main house. Past the fields, in a compound the size of two bull rings, behind the biggest house I've ever been near without pushing a mower, there are bunkhouses and patios and corrals and a stable and everything is painted green with red and white trim. The lawns look like Moody Park in Houston, before the riots, all trimmed and lined with red bricks. The whole place is buzzing with people raking the grass, setting up tables and chairs, painting, and cleaning up. Most of the guys doing the grunt work have shaved heads and my Old Man explains that they are prisoners on work leave from the state pen.

In the center of all the commotion stands a guy wearing a Presidente Rolex with a walky-talky in his hand, barking out orders through a string of cuss words. He's young, in his early thirties, light complexioned, a hundred and eighty pounds with a clean round face behind a long eagle-beaked nose and a trimmed mustache that droops down to frame his stern mouth. He is dressed in a waist-jacketed western suit that looks tailor-made, a 20X felt Stetson, and enough gold around his neck to weigh down a mule. Tucked in his waistband he wears an engraved .38 Colt Super with pearl grips and gold Mexican eagles encrusted on them, strapped in by a leather belt embroidered in maguey fibers called a *cinto piteado*. My Old Man has a belt like this and it cost over five hundred dollars. His boots are made of ostrich skin with his initials etched in gold on each heel.

We follow el Güerro Gil, el Chano, the rest of the guys with AK's, and my Old Man across the compound to the guy with the walkie-talkie. "*Compa* Julio," the man bellows and throws his arms around my Old Man. "I'm so glad you came. You're just in time for the dinner we're giving all the orphaned kids of Durango."

"I'll fit right in with all the orphans," I say as I shake hands with the man my father introduces as el *Comandante* Goyo Fuentes. "I have a father, *pero yo nunca tuve madre.*"

El *Comandante* Goyo busts out laughing and slaps his hand across my back. Every finger has a gold ring, and a two-inch-thick gold bracelet with "*Comandante*" scrolled in diamonds hangs around his wrist. "'*Yo nunca tuve madre,*' that's a good one. This one must give you fits, *Compa* Julio. You should leave him here so he can help me steer these worthless sons of bitches into doing some work." El *Comandante* Goyo reaches out and slaps the shaved head of a guy pushing a wheelbarrow. "*Pinche viejo verga.* You got the whole ranch to work on and you figure it's a good idea to pass by me while I'm welcoming my *compa* and his family. Get your ass away from me before I get *my cuerno de chivo.*" The guy pushing the wheelbarrow trots off spewing apologizes. El *Comandante* Goyo turns back to my Old Man and says, "We're going to kill that bull over there." He points to a grey Brahman bull of about six-hundred pounds standing in a pen. "We got five *bandas* coming and every mariachi we could find in Durango." El *Comandante* Goyo digs into his pocket and pulls out a hundred-dollar bill folded into a "coke pouch," creased lengthwise and folded over with the ends tucked into each other. "We're not going to let Durango sleep for the rest of the week, *compa* Julio." He pulls out a set of keys hanging on a keychain made out of a Mexican *Centenario*, an ounce of pure gold, banded to the chain with a ring of diamonds, and takes one of the keys and scoops up a big hit of coke. He repeats this action a couple of times for each nostril then offers the bill to my Old Man. My Old Man shakes his head and points his chin to me and my brother Junior.

"*No le pones al pase* in front of the kids, *Compa* Julio, that's a good way to be because later *los plebes* want to use *perico* and accuse you of showing them how," el *Comandante* Goyo says folding the bill back up. He holds up his keychain and says, "I can't leave my car at the car wash because the attendants will run off with the keys. The fucking keychain is worth more than the *pinche* Marquis."

"I brought my son Junior in case you needed to get your horses shod," my Old Man says pointing a thumb at Junior.

"Oh, I appreciate that, *compadre*," el *Comandante* Goyo says. He turns to the guys carrying AK's and orders them to take Junior to the stables so he can shoe el *Moro* and el *Alazán* and a few other horses el *comandante* calls by name. I excuse myself and go with Junior to get his gear out of the back of the Magnum while el Chaparro and Beto take turns getting introduced.

"Pretty nice spread," Junior says cinching on his chaps. "Dad says this guy's got some bad-ass horses that can dance to *banda* music like Tony Aguilar's."

"No shit?" I say. "He must be shaking mother-fuckers down left and right. Otherwise how else can a *comandante* afford all this shit?"

"He's not a real *comandante*, *pendejo*. I heard his *charola* is good only in Durango. He can't go all over the country like Dad. Dad's helping to fix this guy up with a badge from the *federales* so he can travel around with his men and not get fucked with for carrying all these guns. Why else do you think we came here?"

I help Junior gather his rasps and clippers from the trunk then turn and eye the group of men carrying AK-47's, strapped with .38's and .45's tucked into the waistbands of their Levis, looking lazily back from under straw Stetsons and Resistol *tejanás* strategically dipped over an eye, and I say, "Fuck, I thought we were going to join *la revolución*."

Junior is trimming the hooves of the third horse while I hold the lead rope and the other guys lean on feed sacks and sit on buckets with their machine guns laying across their laps. El Chano orders one of the prisoners to bring us a tub of Pacífico beer, and I drink enough to make my cheeks feel hot. El Güerro Gil pulls out another hundred-dollar bill full of coke and passes it around. Junior stops shoeing and does a few bumps of coke when the bill reaches him then hands it over to me. I take a heaping bump and then give the bill back to el Güerro Gil. Someone pops the tops off another round of beers, and then I ask if anyone has a joint. This causes everyone but Junior and me to bust out laughing.

"What do you think we have growing in those fields you passed on the way in?" el Chano asks, then slaps a guy called Memo on the back and says, "*Vete por algo bueno en la bodega.*"

"All I saw was *maíz* when we drove in," I say.

"The corn is only a few rows deep. The middle of the fields *están hasta el tronco de mota*," el Chano says.

"Is that safe?" I ask. "I mean any one of those prisoners can wander off into the field to take a crap or something and stumble over the whole crop."

El Güerro Gil laughs and caresses his AK then says, "*Pa' eso son las metralletas.*"

"It was your dad's idea to have us all sworn in as prison guards," el Chano says. "Don Julio helped el *comandante* fix it with the governor and state attorney general so the warden would lend us these prisoners." Chano laughs. "*Plata o plomo, hijo de la chingada*, your dad told them *culeros*."

"And what did they choose?" I ask.

El Guerro Gil looks at his companions and smiles before answering. "*Plata*. We're having the party for the orphans so the governor can come out and get his *mordida*," el Güerro Gil says.

"So you guys aren't really *leyes*?"

The guy called Memo comes back with a bag full of weed just in time to answer me. "*Aquí somos pura maña.*"

"You guys just work in *la movida* like us, and the whole fucking ranch is planted with weed," I say taking a joint from Memo and lighting it. "This is a sweet set up."

"It's a lot better than planting up in the sierra where the soldiers are always marching around or flying over spraying *veneno*," el Chano says.

"All you have to worry about around here is the state police, and you say my Old Man figured a way around that?"

"*Sí, pués, tu papá es muy inteligente.* Aside from the *pinche soldados* starting shit every now and then, we sleep pretty easy around here." El Chano wags his head and pats the AK-47 laying across his lap. "You see how worried they got us."

"And my Old Man is going to help you guys fix the *federales*?" I say holding in a lung full of smoke.

Everyone's face lights up when I say this except for my brother Junior's. Junior is giving me the evil eye for talking so much with these guys, but I can't help it: the cocaine has already taken over.

"When your dad gets us the *charolas* from the *federal*, we can all go back to Sinaloa like *pinche* generals," el Güerro Gil says. He smiles like a guy dreaming of home.

"So you guys aren't even from Durango, hell, you really are *mañosos*," I say and pass the joint to Gil.

Horns and drums blare from outside the stables. El Chano smiles. "*Escucha a la banda.* We sent all the way home to Sinaloa for them," he says and pulls himself up from a bail of hay.

Junior has put up his tools and we are all standing in a circle taking hits of coke off the end of a pocket knife with the sound of *banda* music coming in from the compound. I take a *pase of perico* and pass it to the next guy, then I light a cigarette and wait for the coke to make its way back to me. The bill is only half way around the circle when the *banda* music stops and we hear the sound of crashing wood and people shouting and running feet. Two gunshots are fired then there's this loud fucking bray like a cow got her tits caught on some barbed wire. "*Los soldados,*" el Chano yells. El Güerro Gil, Memo, all those guys, drop the safeties on their AK's and run out of the stables in a "V" formation with el Chano leading the way, his own *cuerno de chivo* at the ready.

Two more shots are fired and there are more crashing sounds by the time Junior and I run out of the stables and find my Old Man. El Chano and the rest of the guys are standing in a half circle behind my Dad and el *Comandante* Goyo. El *comandante* takes aim and fires another double shot into the Brahman bull standing in the middle of a bunch of broken up tables and chairs and shouts, "*allí cae.*" But the fucking bull doesn't fall; it just keeps on smashing shit up. Red and black dots appear on the bull's neck and shoulder and the bull wails again with its tongue sticking out long and bloody as two more bullets rip into him. The bull, probably alarmed by the *banda* music, has somehow broken out of his pen and is now ransacking the area where the tables and chairs are set up. Workers are running around trying to avoid the bull and the *comandante's* line of fire at the same time. Someone throws a rope around the bull's neck and the bull charges when it feels the noose tighten. The prisoner at the end of the rope breaks his hold but not before burning the shit out of his hands. He comes running up to *Comandante* Goyo holding out his palms showing the two bloody grooves the rope had opened up, and el *Comandante* Goyo slaps him across the mouth. "*Pinche viejo verga.* Who told you to butt in?"

El *Comandante* Goyo takes the AK away from el Chano and empties the clip into the bull. The bull staggers under the thumping of the bullets then falls to its knees. The blood streams out its nose and mouth then it crumples over and stops breathing altogether.

"¿*Dónde 'stá el pinche Sapo*?" el *Comandante* Goyo shouts. "I left that stupid son of a bitch in charge of that bull."

A man with an Uzi hanging off his shoulder runs up yelling, "Here I am, *jefe*."

"*Hijo de tu chingada madre*, didn't I tell you to take care of that bull? What the fuck were you doing?" El *comandante* tears the man called Sapo's hat off and throws it to the ground. "You go and get me another bull you *pinche pendejo* before I serve your balls to the orphans."

"Sí *jefe*, right away *jefe*," el Sapo says turning to leave, then stops. "Why can't we just cook this bull since it's already dead?"

"*Idiota*," el *Comandante* Goyo says. "I'm not going to serve a bunch of orphans meat that's been all shot up. *Hijo de tu chingada madre*, don't you think those *pobrecitos* have suffered enough?"

The next day we leave Durango in three separate cars. Junior and el Chaparo leave first in the Dodge Magnum. They're driving straight to Reynosa so Junior can cross into the U.S. and go back to his home outside of Dallas with the three thousand dollars el *comandante* gave him for shoeing the horses. Before we leave Durango, el *comandante* gives us all embroidered belts like his and promises to have ostrich boots made in our sizes by the time we come back. My Old Man promises to bring back four AK-47's in a few weeks.

My father and Beto ride in a brand new cherry red Chevy pick-up el *Comandante* Goyo is sending as a gift to a for-real *comandante* my dad knows. I follow behind in a grey '78 special edition Monte Carlo. The Chevy pick-up is stolen but el *comandante* says the Monte Carlo is straight and that my Old Man can have it. El Chano made el Memo roll me about twenty joints for the road before we lit out. I enjoy riding alone past the gorged earth and through the sierra, skirting ridges that break off at the road's edge into cliffs. I light a joint and gun the Monte

Carlo after my Old Man in the red Chevy, wondering who the fuck do we know in Guadalajara. Then I remember that Steely Dan song and I figure that in my case Guadalajara will have to do.

Chapter VI

Instead of going back toward Torreón, I follow my Old Man and Beto out of Durango southwest to Mazatlán. I want to go to the beach while we're there, but my Old Man tells me that the best he can do for me is let me turn a few cartwheels at the gas station while we refuel if I'm "so excited to see a fucking ocean." We go along the coast down to Villa Union then to Escuinapa—just like the *caballo blanco* José Alfredo Jiménez sings about in that *corrido*, only we're going south and the horse in the ballad was heading north. Alongside the road, banana trees, palms, and elephant ear ivies grow like madness. We leave Escuinapa and start making our way up the sierra just as it gets dark. The temperature drops fifteen degrees in as many minutes.

Nobody tells me where we're going next or if we're going to stop and sleep before we get there. I don't ask. I just act like I know what I'm doing like everyone else in the world. This trip is part of those "big things" Beto was talking about. Big things call for big secrets, but I've never heard of any secret that's been kept for long.

We drive through Acaponeta, Tecuala, Rosamo-rado, and Tuxpan, eating up little towns all the way to Tepic, Nayarit—where el Chaparro lost that load of weed. We refuel in Tepic. There's a kitchen open at the station, and Beto and I go in and buy coffee. When we come out with our coffees, my Old Man is talking to these guys driving a white Grand Marquis with no plates. The Marquis has tinted windows, custom rims, and I can hear the distinct squawk of radio chatter so I know they're *Federales*. My Old Man shakes hands with the driver. I only catch a glimpse of the driver's arm and the side of his head before the window goes up and the car pulls out of the gas station.

My Old Man walks over to us and says, "*Ya 'stá*," and then tells me to get in the Monte Carlo and follow behind the Feds. He pulls in behind me, and we drive with me sandwiched between the Chevy and the Marquis out of Tepic and down the dark sierra.

From Tepic we hit Ixtlan del Río. The Marquis is passing cars like they're standing still and I'm right on its taillights. The Marquis runs blocker for me and stays in the oncoming traffic lane while I make my pass so I can be sure the lane is clear and pass double-trailer rigs around curves and over hills with no danger of hitting anything head on. Down every valley and at all the cross roads there are checkpoints manned with AK-47-toting Feds and crews of *madrinas* eager to pick our cars apart in search of drugs, weapons, or anything else that might mean cash. The Marquis stops at each checkpoint and doesn't move till my car and my Old Man behind me are past the guns, then speeds up to regain the lead on the road through the sierra. We skirt Tequila, Jalisco, and just as dawn hits, drive straight into Guadalajara and to el Hotel Las Américas on the edge of town.

Four guys get out of the Marquis. I recognize Armando Espinoza, Polo Remejorado, and Rafael Ronco, but I don't know the fourth guy. I walk over and say hello.

"*¿Qué onda, hijo?*" Armando says and gives me a hug. "You stayed right with me *sin jotiar*."

"*¿Qué pasó, Armando-broncas?* I thought you knew you had an international wheel man behind you." Armando is new to the *clicka* that makes up el *comandante* Jorge Torres del Rey's "*grupo especial.*" I've known these guys for as long as I can remember except for Armando, whom I met only a few years ago. He dresses out at about two-fifty and wears a big handlebar mustache. Armando is from Oaxaca, but he's been in Mexico City so long that he talks like a *chilango.*

I turn and greet Rafael Ronco or Don Gato as we all call him. "*¿Qué habido, mí top cat?* You guys still fighting crime?"

Don Gato stops chewing on his tongue and strokes his mustache so that I catch a glimpse of his bottom lip then fixes his coke-bottle glasses and says, "We're making the criminals pay, that's for sure."

"Paying *mordidas,*" Polo says, "For looking the other way when something may or may not be happening." Polo pulls up his pants and secures the gun in his waistband. "But we never aid in any criminal activity. We are not baggage handlers like the *pinche* state police."

"Someone's got to fund *la Policía Judicial Federal,*" Armando says.

"*Oye a este animal. La Policía Federal* is funded by the government," Polo says. "We collect fines for crimes that will or will not be determined later." Polo is short and light complexioned and wears tiny wire-framed glasses. He looks a lot like a nerdy high school kid except he has a gun and talks to people like he wants a chance to use it. "You know nothing about the law, Armando."

"Where's Memo and the *comandante?* Are they staying here at this hotel?" I ask.

"They'll be back later," Polo says. "They're making sure some guys we detained sleep warm tonight."

Armando laughs. "You should see the *pinche indios* we picked up. I must have shot half a truck load of mineral water up their noses, and they still wouldn't tell us where they had their *mota* planted."

Shooting mineral water up a suspect's nose is standard procedure for *federales*. Anyone who gets picked up by the *federales* will be blindfolded, handcuffed, and laid on their back. Then some guy sits on the prisoner's chest and stuffs a rag down his throat. The gag is just to prevent the *detenido* from breathing through his mouth; the Feds couldn't give a fuck if anyone hears a prisoner scream. I think the Feds like to hear the screams. The mineral water is then shaken—some really medieval fuckers put chile pepper into the mineral water—and shot up the detainee's nose where he can't help but drown on the agitated soda for the couple of minutes it takes for the fizz to run out. Guys have told me that when the mineral water shoots up the nose and hits the base of the neck it feels like the soul is ripped from the body. While the detainee finishes convulsing and gagging on the club soda, the cattle prod—called the *chicharra* because it sounds like a cicada humming when activated—is used on the balls to wake the prisoner out of the drowning sensation. This process is repeated over and over until the prisoner confesses to whatever he is being charged with.

The guy sitting on the prisoner's chest usually isn't a commissioned fed or a *ciento tres* like they call each other in their radio code. The *federales* always have guys working for them called *madrinas*, godmothers, who administer the beatings. *Madrinas* are pseudo-cops who do all the dirty work, frisking cars, shaking down guys at checkpoints, and of course administering "*las calentadas.*" Torres's men don't use *madrinas* to do their dirty work, and I guess that's what makes them "*el grupo especial.*"

"Hey, who's the guy riding with you? The one talking to my dad."

"That's the *comandante's* brother, Gerardo," Don Gato says.

"Is he in charge while the *Comanche* is out?"

"He thinks he is," Don Gato says. "We just brought him along to flash at the checkpoints."

I've known Don Gato for years, way back to when he, Polo, Memo, and el *comandante* Torres del

Rey were all in jail in Tijuana for killing a Mexican Customs agent. My Old Man used to take me down to TJ when I was a kid and we'd visit these guys in jail and take them candies and shampoo. The *comandante* and his group were able to fix their way out of jail and back into being *Federales*. Lately I've been hearing about Torres del Rey getting promoted to *Segundo Comandante de la Nación*. This places him directly under the *Primer Comandante de la Republica* who takes orders only from the Attorney General, who only takes orders from el *Presidente*. And even though I know all this shit already, Beto explains it to me in great detail—like he just discovered the fucking new world—after I introduce him to the guys and we're unloading our luggage from the back of the Monte Carlo.

The *comandante's* brother Gerardo comes walking over to us with his arm draped around my Old Man's shoulder. "I could only get two extra rooms because they're having some convention or wedding *chingadera*. You guys will have to share a room so Don Julio can use the other one."

"That's okay," my Old Man says. "I'll sleep with these guys. Save the room for my *compadre* when he gets in later."

"But I'm going to send for some whores," Gerardo says.

"Let el Johnny have mine," my Old Man says taking a hotel key from Gerardo. "Beto you better get that '*encargo*' out of the car."

Beto looks around and says, "Right here?" Aside from a chamber maid sweeping the sidewalk on the other side of the parking lot in front of the reception, there is no one stirring at the hotel.

"You afraid someone might call the police?" my Old Man asks.

Beto drops his luggage on the spot and elbows me to follow him to the Monte Carlo. He opens the door and pushes the front seat down and starts pulling out the back seat.

"Go pull on the other side," Beto says.

I hustle around the other side of the car and we pry the backseat out. Under the seat are four bundles the size of hat boxes, only not as tall, wrapped in cellophane.

"Hey, Beto this isn't weed," I whisper through clenched teeth. "These are fucking stacks of hundred dollar bills."

"*No hagas tanto pedo,*" Beto says handing me another bundle and then picking up the other two.

We walk at a clip, carrying the money cradled in our arms like it was firewood, over to the open door where my Old Man is standing and enter the suite. Beto opens the closet door with his foot. We stack the bundles and close the door just as Armando, Don Gato, Polo, and Gerardo come in with our luggage. Armando opens the closet and decides there's no room for our luggage and flings our bags to a corner. Armando throws himself down on one of the double beds and grabs the phone off the nightstand.

"I'm ordering some tortas from room service," Armando says.

"*¿Cómo qué* tortas? *Animal,*" Don Gato says. "This is a five-star hotel. Order something classy like a club sandwich."

"It's the same fucking thing," Armando says. "A *mojado* spends one summer in Chicago washing dishes and suddenly he's a culinary expert."

My Old Man sits down at a table by the door with Polo and Don Gato. Gerardo says he's got a bottle of whiskey in his room and goes off to get it. Beto says something about fixing the car seat and I follow him out.

"Why didn't you fuckers tell me there was all that money under the seat?" I ask as I catch up to Beto by the parking lot.

"What would you have done if you knew you had a half a million dollars under your seat?" Beto starts wedging the back seat into place.

"I would've lost you guys in Mazatlán," I say, and push down on my end of the seat.

"You would've worried yourself off the edge of the sierra, that's what you would've done."

"Is all that money going to el *comandante* Torres?"

"Some of it is. Most of it is going up to the *Procurador* so he can sign off on some federal badges for *Comandante* Goyo Fuentes and his men," Beto says. "But what we care about is that your dad's *compadre* Torres is *segundo comandante* now and he can send a friend of your dad's as *comandante* to Reynosa. I heard your dad say Gus Maniobra is going to be *comandante* in Reynosa when we get back."

"I know el Goose. He's a tall fucker. He calls my dad *Apa*," I say, happy to know at least what all this means. "We're going to have the *plaza* aren't we Beto?" This is it, the big leagues. The guy who holds the *plaza* has a direct hotline to the *comandante* of the federal and all the other law enforcement agencies in town. Some guy gets busted with a load, all we have to do is call the *comandante* and he's out and we have a load on the cheap. Someone wants to cut a deal for a few tons of weed to go through town, we call the *comandante* and bam, police escort all the way to the river. The guy who holds the *plaza* handles the pay-offs to the Feds, and all the state and municipal cops have to fall in line and take the chump change. We're going to run Reynosa now.

"This is just a start," Beto says. "For right now the *Procurador* is as high as we can fix, but soon Johnny, real soon, we'll be able to fix things even higher than that."

"But for now we're fixing the who?"

"The *Procurador*, the Attorney General of the Republic. Come on Johnny, you're going to be a law student soon. You have to learn these terms," Beto says. "But don't worry about the money; we'll get a little bit of it too."

"I think I'd rather go work for the *Procurador* if he's pulling in that kind of cash."

"Johnny, study hard and get a degree, and someday you'll be the Attorney General."

Back in the suite, Armando orders tortas, club sandwiches, chilaquiles, huevos rancheros, carne asada, queso—eight of everything. We wash breakfast down with two cups of coffee then switch to beer and whiskey. After the chambermaid clears the table and brings more beer and the set up for the whiskey, we pull the mattresses off the box springs. Everyone grabs a spot to lie down and puts his gun within arm's reach or under his pillow. I don't have a gun so I unfold my knife and slide it under my pillow. We sleep till evening when the ring of the telephone wakes me.

Don Gato picks up the receiver and says, "¿Qué? Sí. Ya vamos."

Armando, Polo, and Don Gato check their guns and leave with my dad. Beto and I push the mattresses back on the box springs and start watching TV. A half hour later, Gerardo knocks on our door—he must have left after I fell asleep—and walks in with three women following behind him.

"The whores are here," Gerardo says. "Where did everyone go?"

"I think Don Rafa and the others got a call from the comandante and they went out," Beto says. "Maybe we should hold off on the party until Don Julio and the rest return."

"Ah, no, Don Julio said Johnny could have his whore," Gerardo says. "Go ahead, Johnny, take your pick."

Two of the women are sitting on the bed. The woman next to Gerardo is wearing a red jumpsuit with a zipper down the front. Gerardo pulls down the zipper and bares her chest down to her black lace bra. Gerardo jumps up and pulls the other woman off the bed. She is more slender than the woman in the jumpsuit and taller. Gerardo lifts her dress and bends her over so I can see her ass.

"How 'bout this one, Johnny? Now that's an ass," Gerardo says, then moves toward the girl sitting at the table. The girl at the table gets up and holds off Gerardo.

"I'll do it," she says and unties a strap that's wrapped around her waist. Her dress unfolds and she stands with it open in her bra and panties. Gerardo and the two other whores are whooping and cheering like someone hit a home run and the girl in her underwear begins to dance for them.

I look at Beto and he shrugs, then calls me over to one side.

Beto says, "Go ahead and have a good time. Your dad said you'd done well on the road. I'm sure he'd want to do something nice for you if he were here."

"Really? My Old Man said I did good on the road? When did he say this, in the truck?"

"Let's just say he had more good things than bad to say about your driving."

I call a cab and have it take me and the girl who danced in her underwear to el Hotel Malibu—you can't be with a whore in a room full of money; they tell their pimps everything. It's a nice hotel built like a Spanish mission. The hotel forms a square around a courtyard that's lined by banana trees and hanging plants and vines crawling up the sides of the building. The rooms are spread out on two floors and topped with a red tile roof. We get a room next to the parking lot on the second floor with a balcony looking over a garden. There's a king-sized bed and the bathroom has a tub with legs shaped like eagle claws. I phone the front desk to connect me to the Hotel Las Américas. I get Beto on the line and tell him what hotel and room I'm in, then I order six whiskeys. The girl brings a highball over to me then kicks off her shoes and unwraps herself out of her dress. She goes into the bathroom wearing only her bra and panties. I can hear her running water and flushing the toilet as I strip off my clothes and turn off the lights. When she comes out of the bathroom, she is carrying a roll of toilet paper that she places on the nightstand. I'm lying down in only my boxer shorts with my arms folded behind my head.

"Do you want me now?" she says and turns the light back on. "I'm glad I'm with you tonight. When my friends told me we were going to a party with *comandante* Torres, I thought they meant Torres Conde."

"I know that guy," I say. "He's a *comandante* in the *Federal*. But he's not my Dad's *compadre*."

"All he likes to do is wear my underwear. I'm glad I'm with a young good-looking man tonight."

"Oh man, you're getting a big tip." I pull her down on top of me and start kissing her neck and shoulders. She rolls off me and slips out of her panties and undoes her bra. She lies naked—only she doesn't call it being naked, she calls it being *bichy*—with her legs open and I push myself in. I'm humping away but I don't know when to cum because this is the first time I'm with a woman where I don't have someone knocking on the door telling me time's up. After a while, she rolls me over and straddles me and rocks back and forth till I cum. She reaches over and grabs the roll of toilet paper while she's still mounted on me. She wraps paper around her hand then reaches under her and grabs me by the base of my cock. She runs her hand with the toilet paper up my cock as she pulls herself off. She makes a final swipe with the toilet paper around the head of my dick then wads the tissue up and stuffs it in her crotch. She sits on her knees for a while and then says, "There, that should be all of it." Then she gets up and waddles to the bathroom holding the wadded up toilet paper between her legs. All whores clean dicks and themselves like this, but this is the first time I've seen it done in the light.

We make love all night. At times I doze off only to wake up and crawl back on her. The whore is really nice and receives me with kisses and giggles every time I mount her. We're still going at it when the chambermaid comes in with her pass key to clean up the room the next morning. The whore tells me she has to go. After she gets dressed I offer to tip her. She says that Gerardo wouldn't like it and that she hopes I call her again sometime. I order a steak and huevos rancheros after the whore leaves. When the chambermaid comes to pick up the dirty dishes, I apologize for what she saw earlier.

"You don't have to be embarrassed," she says. "You get used to seeing things like that after you work here for a while."

I ask her to join me for a cup of coffee and she comes over and takes a seat next to me on the foot of the bed. I scoot my hand over and take hers, and she leans in for me to kiss her. I cover her mouth with mine, and we stay like this till I move my hands up her dress and she pushes me away. I pull out all the money I have in my pockets and hand it out to her. The maid jumps up from the bed knocking over the coffee table I was breakfasting on and runs out of the room crying. I finish getting dressed and leave the room without checking out.

Back at the hotel, *comandante* Torres del Rey is tearing his brother Gerardo a new asshole. I hear the *comandante* yelling even before Don Gato opens the door for me. My Old Man is lying on one of the double beds with his arms folded behind his head watching TV—he doesn't return my greeting. Gerardo is sitting at the table, head bowed, and the *comandante* is standing over him.

It's real funny to see the *comandante* mad because he looks just like the guy who plays *Chespirito* and el *Chavo del Ocho* on TV. His round face, droopy cheeks, and pickaxe nose make him look like he's in a constant state of confusion, but the *comandante* is sharp and he doesn't take any shit. I saw the *comandante* split a guy's head open with his pistol for flicking his cigarette ashes on the table cloth while we were having lunch one day.

"*¿No ves, hijo de tu chingada madre?*" el *comandante* says in a thick *chilango* accent. "What do you think would happen if a reporter came by while you were parading whores around the hotel? Don't you see *la prensa* is just waiting for a chance to put my face on the front page of some scandal?" The *comandante* notices me standing in the doorway and says, "I've been waiting to talk to you. Where the fuck've you been?"

"I was legged up with a whore at the Malibu."

The *comandante* looks at me like he is trying to decide if I am of the torturable classes and says, "Legged up with some whore, well at least you had enough sense to go to a different hotel. I'll deal with you in a moment." The *comandante* turns back to Gerardo and says, "He's got enough sense to go to a different hotel. Get your worthless self back to Mexico City before I forget we have the same mother and give you a *calentada* just like we do to any son of a bitch *que no pone el culo derecho.*"

"I'll just get my things and go then," Gerardo says, his eyes filling with tears.

"You'll go now like I said," the *comandante* says chest-bumping Gerardo to the door. "I've given you everything you have and you aren't taking shit, you hear me *imbécil?*" The *comandante* stands in the doorway cussing at Gerardo.

I go over to Don Gato and ask if the *comandante* is pissed off at me. Don Gato says, "El *comandante* isn't even mad about the whores. He's just getting rid of the dead weight before he starts passing out shares of the money you brought."

I'm about to explain that I didn't even know the money was stashed in the car but right then the *comandante* turns to me and says, *"Hola, hijo,* can't you come over here and greet me properly, or do you think because you bring me a bundle of money you can treat me like a *puta?"*

I cross the room and shake the *comandante's* hand, and he pulls me into a hug. The *comandante* squeezes me to his chest and slaps his hand down hard on my back several times before he releases me.

"Gracias, hijo," the *comandante* says. "I appreciate what you've done for us. Armando and everyone have told me how you rode down here all by yourself through checkpoints and sierra without pissing your pants. You have balls the size of your father's and I'm not going to let that go unrewarded. I wanted to be the one to buy you the best whore in Guadalajara but since that piece of shit brother of mine has stolen even that pleasure from me, I'm going to give you a car." The *comandante* turns to my Old Man and says, "If it's all right with my *compadre* of course."

He takes his eyes off the TV for a second and nods then goes back to watching the news.

"Wow, thanks *comandante,*" I say and even though I try to fight it, I get choked up. "Everyone is being *buena onda* and everything and I appreciate the car, but I just did what I was told and—."

"And nothing," the *comandante* says. "I'm buying my son, Jorgito, a new car and you're getting his old one. It's a good car. It's the one you boys took to Acapulco last summer. Jorgito said you liked the car, and he'll be glad when he hears it's you that's getting it."

My Old Man swings his legs off the bed, takes his hat off the night stand, eases it on, and pulls down on the front and back until he is satisfied with the fit. He gets up and walks over to me and puts his arm across my shoulders and says, "You've fucked something other than your fist and the *comandante* just gave you your cut, so get yourself a drink before we head back home and let me finish talking with my *compadre*." He opens the door and says to Torres, "We can finish our talk now *compadre*."

The *comandante* takes his hands out of his leisure suit, clicks his heels in attention: "As you say *compadre*." The *comandante* turns before he follows my Old Man out of the suite and says, "I'll send for each of you one by one as soon as my *compadre* and I have finished our talk. If my wife or the *Procurador* calls, send it to room 114. Take a message if it's anyone else."

Don Gato shuts the door behind the *comandante* and Armando hands me a whiskey highball.

"How was the whore, Johnny?" Polo says from the bed.

"She was great, never once looked at her watch," I say then take a pull from my drink. "I got to fuck the chamber maid too; she was young."

"*No mames*," Polo says. "You didn't fuck the maid. You can't fuck any girl from Jalisco on the first date. You can't lie to the *Federal*."

"I kissed her."

Don Gato stands in front of me and stops chewing on his tongue to smile and stare at me with bloodshot eyes made even larger and redder by the thickness of his glasses. "You missed all the fun last night, Johnny. We made Armando a priest."

I turn to Armando. "No shit, Armando, I didn't even know you went to church. Did you have to pay off a cardinal or something?"

"The guys we picked up a few days ago wouldn't tell us where they had their pot planted or give up any money from what they'd already harvested," Polo says. "Hardheaded *Michoacanos*, these guys. I was just about to start shooting kneecaps when Memo shows up with a priest's robe. Armando gets into the robe then takes the blindfold off one of the detainees."

"You should've seen that guy's face when he saw me standing in front of him dressed like a *cura*," Armando says. "*Pinche indio* thought I was there to give him his last rites. I calm him down and start telling him how *papá diosito* is mad at him for growing pot. I tell him he might go to hell and the fucking indian starts crying and starts singing so much about who he's paying off for his patch that I have to slap the shit out of him to shut him up."

Don Gato laughs hard then takes off his glasses and rubs his eyes. "The poor little indian kept asking me why *el señor cura* got so mad."

"We got the patch where they had their pot planted and made them cough up all the cash they had," Polo says rubbing his palms together.

"What are you guys going to do with all that pot?" I ask.

"We have to burn some of it for the newspapers, but I'm sure you'll get the rest up there in Reynosa when it's finished drying," Armando says.

"So did you let the guys go?"

The smile disappears from Polo's face and he says, "No. Memo's taking them to headquarters for booking right now. *¿De cual fumaste*, Johnny? What'd you think we'd do with them?"

"I don't know, I thought you'd let 'em go since you got what you wanted," I say. "What happens after the booking?"

Beto gets up from the bed and says, "They will be turned over to the D.A. then to the judge and receive no less than seven years in prison for committing *delitos contra la salud.*"

I turn to Don Gato and he's chewing on his tongue nodding to everything Beto says.

"So, you guys beat the shit out of these guys for a few days, take their cash and their pot, scare them into thinking they're going to hell for all eternity, *and* you still send them to jail for years?"

"Yeah," Don Gato says pushing up his glasses.

"But they gave you everything you wanted, why'd you have to send them to jail?"

Don Gato hunches his shoulders and spreads his palms in front of him and says, "That's our job."

The phone rings and Polo answers it. Polo hangs up the phone without ever speaking a word and says, "Armando, you're up first."

Armando slaps his hands together and lets out a *grito* then leaves the room. I go over and sit on the bed where my Old Man had been lying and watch each one of the Feds go out and receive their cut of the half a million dollars el *Comandante* Goyo— the guy who holds special dinners for orphans and grows pot practically on the side of the road—sent from Durango.

Chapter VII

On our way back from Guadalajara, we stop in Monterrey and see about getting me into law school. The main office of the *Sindicato de Aduana* is a one-story Spanish-tiled house in San Pedro, a suburb of Monterrey. There are two desks set up in what must have been the living room. The kitchen counters are lined with whiskey bottles, four thick, standing in puddles of melted ice and spilt booze. The dining area, and from what I see on my way to the bathroom every other room in the house, is filled with VCRs, TVs, kitchen appliances, and all sorts of *falluca* stacked shoulder high and wall to wall.

Roberto Pequeño sits across a glass topped desk from my father nodding and twitching to everything my Old Man says. He has a handkerchief in his hand, and he's working it all over his face and head. He dabs it over his forehead, where the hair has receded, and then begins to work it down over his wrinkled brow. He takes the corner of the kerchief and pokes it into the darkened sockets that house dilated pupils flickering in all directions as if trying to avoid contact with the yellow film that covers the rest of the eye. Then he needles the cloth down over his red nose and across his flushed cheeks, going around the rim of his mouth, down his chin, and around both sides of his neck. It's like watching a cat lick itself clean. He's fucked up on cocaine, but then again so is my Old Man.

My Dad's grinding his teeth, taking shots of whiskey straight from the bottle, and explaining in the nicest way his condition will allow how much he would *appreciate* Pequeño's help getting me into law school. My Old Man ends his request staring across the desk with eyes that look like they're about to pop out of their sockets, nostrils flaring, and every tooth in his head showing. I'm sitting here thinking that I got Mr. Hyde and Mr. Hyde as my references to get into college, and my Dr. Jekyll, Beto Prietón, instead of being the voice of reason, just sits there gnawing at his fingernails like it's the only thing in the world he's got to do. Then suddenly, Pequeño says, "Of course, of course, it would be an honor." Then he picks up the phone and starts making calls. By the third number and a half hour wait for a call back, I'm set to meet with the guy who knows the other guy at Admissions at the *Universidad Autónoma de Nuevo León.*

We're shaking hands, making for the door with names and contacts to get me into school, and Pequeño goes and says, "Say hi to your *compadre* Lolo for me when you see him."

My Old Man's eyes light up, and his cheeks crease into what a stranger might call a smile. "We're heading that way. I think I'll stop by and pay him a visit."

Ah, fuck. We have no reason to go into Los Ramones. Even after we took the sheep, we'd already gone back twice. The first time, my Old Man saw Lolo crossing the *plaza* and went over and cussed him out right there in front of the whole town. That should've been enough. I mean we succeeded in embarrassing Lolo, and it wasn't like we were hurting for money since we had sold that key and were getting other deals done. But we went into Los Ramones again after that, and this time my Old Man caught Lolo at

Chema's cantina. I had to stand by the door and not let anyone in or out while Dad slapped the shit out of his *compadre*, leaving him lying in a pool of spilt beer. Now we're going to Los Ramones for no fucking reason other than to *chingar* Lolo again. I'm only a couple of phone calls away from getting into college. I can be showered and at Cynthia's house in a few hours. All my Old Man has to do is get home and wait for Torres to name el Goose *comandante* in Reynosa and he'll have the *plaza*. We have every reason in the world to get home and no need whatsoever to shake down Lolo, but for Dad and every other Mexican in the world, success ain't shit if you can't use it to step all over people, so we're going to Los Ramones.

Beto steers the Monte Carlo north on HWY 2 out of San Pedro. After sixty kilometers and at least four hits of coke disguised as desperate searches through the glove box, my Old Man tells Beto to hang a left at the *entronque*, the café/bus station that sits on the corner of HWY 2 and the road that leads to Los Ramones. We barely get over the concrete slab that passes for a bridge crossing el Río Pesquería and there's Lolo with a bunch of guys drinking beer under a big mesquite tree and a *conjunto* pumping out *corridos*. My Old Man gets out of the car before Beto has a chance to bring it to a full stop.

My Old Man passes through the ring of men around Lolo—most of them I recognize as Lolo's drivers—and grabs hold of his *compadre*'s outstretched hand and pulls him into a hug. A wave of relief flushes over Lolo's face followed by an uncertain smile that makes him look like he's pissing through a case of the clap.

"*Compadre de mi vida*," Lolo says. "What brings you here?"

"I wanted to hear some music," my Old Man says then orders the *conjunto*, "Play 'Pedro Avilés.'"

I'm pulling a chicken wing off the grill when the first strands of the *corrido* start up. I nearly gag on the chicken. "Pedro Avilés" is a song about this hired gun. It starts off, *Usted dira general, pa' los trompos son las cuerdas.* For a northern Mexican, those words are a call out, a way of saying, "only bad asses can throw down." As the *conjunto* finishes the first few chords, everybody under the mesquite tree starts to step slowly, conspicuously, back away from the two *compadres* standing knee high in chaparral with the brims of their straw Panamas almost touching each other. The *conjunto* finishes the song, and my Old Man orders them to play it again. Lolo is consumed by nervous laughter that comes out dry and hoarse.

"You trying to learn that song, *compadre*?"

"I just like what it says."

By the time the *conjunto* finishes playing "Pedro Avilés" for the third time, *norteños* in every sort of good or poor western wear are pulling up under the mesquite in pick ups, taxis, horses, and bicycles, grabbing positions on rocks, tailgates, crowding over each other, elbows jutting out for an extra bit of space, stretching their necks over shoulders for their chance to see my Old Man's next move.

I hear a voice in my ear say, "Lolo's had it now." I look up and see my dad's cousin, Tío Raúl, standing over me, running a calloused finger over his salt-and-pepper mustache.

"When'd you get here?"

Tío Raúl pushes his stained straw hat up and wipes a bandana over his face and shrugs, never taking his eyes off of Lolo and my Old Man. My Old Man seems amused by everything Lolo says and shows it by bellowing fits of laughter that he accents by clapping Lolo hard on the shoulders and punching at his arms. Lolo makes no attempt to play down how heavy my Old Man's hand is and he winces and moans after each punch.

"Do you think they're going to fight?"

My tío Raúl coughs into his fist and lets out a low, "Shhhh." And then I notice that, aside from the *conjunto's* playing, the crowd has grown as silent as an alley after a murder. I see Lolo's son, Andrés, break away from the crowd and walk up to his father. Beto trails a couple of meters behind Andrés. I can hear only bits of what Andrés is saying: "Please . . *amigos* . . *toda la vida* . . *mís respectos*."

Lolo staggers back away from my Old Man and his son like a drunk trying to fight off restraint. He hurls his beer to one side and pulls a .38 Super out of his waistband yelling, "*Yo también soy hombre.*"

In one frantic motion, while drawing his own gun, my Old Man wraps an arm around Andrés's neck, pulling him in. Lolo's knees buckle when he sees his son in my Old Man's grasp. Beto chambers a bullet, and the sound makes Lolo lose focus on my Old Man and turn for just a second. There's a crack from my Old Man's .38 and the air is ripped and shattered into a million screaming pieces as Lolo's gun goes flying in the air and a red speck appears on his brow. Lolo puts his fingers to the wound and brings his hands down and looks at his bloodstained fingers like he's just seen them for the first time. Then he faints.

The rubberneckers under the mesquite tree simultaneously make a break in every direction except toward where Lolo falls. The musicians are splashing across the knee high waters of the Río Pesquería holding *tololoches*, accordions, and guitars over their heads. There's a guy running behind a pick-up truck trying to climb into the bed but the driver isn't slowing down. Guys are losing their hats running through the chaparral, advancing a few meters then falling face first and disappearing in the brush only to reappear and continue on their headlong sprint.

My Old Man pushes his gun under Andrés's chin and says, "What are you driving?" Andrés points a limp arm at a black Chevy Silverado and my Old Man guides him toward it. Beto picks up Lolo's gun and holds it up showing the dented barrel where my Old Man's bullet hit. He moves around the truck and slips behind the wheel, sandwiching Andrés between him and my Old Man. They take off in the truck. I run a few meters behind them till I'm standing in the middle of the road watching the taillights bounce over ruts and potholes then disappear around a bend, waiting for my Old Man to turn around, to at least look back, but he never does.

Chapter VIII

I'm now starting law school, and I need a place to stay. Turns out my Old Man has this family living in Monterrey he visits when he passes through the city. I think it's the family he always wanted if he hadn't got stuck with us. The mother used to go to school with him and he was sweet on her when they were kids. This lady, *la tía* Virginia, has three kids now, but the oldest son has already married and moved out. The father is an engineer for a steel company and is able to provide a modest home for his family, but not enough to match the gifts my Old Man brings when he visits. Tía Gina's other son, Poncho, is my age and my Old Man figures he's a good friend for me. Poncho's a brat who doesn't work or study and throws tantrums when his mother refuses to give him money to go out drinking with his buddies. There's a daughter too, Claudia, but she prefers to be called Clau. She's a year younger than me and she is smoking hot. She has a nice full round ass and real perky boobs, wild curly brown hair, big cow eyes with thick lashes, beautiful lips, and perfect teeth. But she's more of a brat than

Poncho. Claudia's always slinking around my Old Man giving it the old "Tío Julio, I just love watching movies on the VCR you brought me," or, "Tío Julio, have you heard about CD players, they're just the most marvelous thing." I move into big brother Fito's old room and start law school at the *Centro de Estudios Universitarios de Monterrey*.

Cynthia is not at all happy about me studying in Monterrey. She says she doesn't like having to wait till the weekends to go out and she is positive that I will find some "other *pendeja*" and marry her after I become a lawyer. Cynthia keeps saying, "*novia de estudiante nunca será esposa de profesionista.*" I can't believe she's even considering marrying me, and I don't have the words to explain to her that there's no one else I'd rather fuck for the rest of my life than her. I manage to calm her down by leaving her spending money every week and telling her to save as much as she can of the dough so we can get married when I finish school.

I fumble around Monterrey for the first semester of my studies. There're a lot of guys I know from Reynosa studying law, criminology, medicine, architecture, clothing design, engineering, agriculture, or anything else their folks can afford. I waste several months hanging out with a few of these guys because they're familiar faces. Real soon, it's clear that the guys from Reynosa are just as out of place as I am and have a lot more practical problems too. They don't know their way around town, they never have any spending money, and they don't know how to hustle a buck other than to call home for their parents to send them money. At best these Reynosa guys can point me in the direction of a good taco stand. They're boozers, broke boozers at that, and are useless to me for scoring weed.

This one night, I go out with a couple of guys I know from Reynosa, Rudy el Gordo and Pepe Elías. We're popping in and out of bars around the *macro-plaza* near *la zona hotelera* in the *pueblo viejo* district, having a couple of rounds at each stop before deciding we can't pick up any girls, then moving to the next bar. By the third or fourth bar, I'm feeling pretty lit. I only have two gears when I drink, happy and mad. On this night, I'm mad. I keep getting stuck with the tab. We stumble into this bohemian bar that has a band playing some kind of Guatemalan jungle music, mostly pan pipes and bongos. I like the sound but el Gordo and Pepe Elías keep calling it *mariguano* music and saying we should leave.

"One of you pay the tab and we'll leave," I say.

"You get this one, and we'll get the next one," Pepe Elías says.

"You guys haven't stuck your hands in your pockets all night."

"So, you've got money, what's the problem?" el Gordo says.

"I've got to get through the rest of the week just like you guys."

"You can just call home and get your dad to send you more," el Gordo says spreading his hands and giving it the "this fucking guy" look.

"I'm not calling my Old Man and telling him I'm out of cash because I wasted my money buying my friends drinks."

"Why would he care?" Pepe Elías says.

"Yeah, it's not like anyone has to work for the cash," el Gordo says.

"What the fuck do you guys think my Old Man does for his money?"

"Come on, we all know he's a *mañoso*," Pepe Elías says.

"So? You don't think that's work?" I say. "You think it's easy dealing with the Feds? You guys think the guns are there just to accessorize?"

"Yeah, but he doesn't have a real job like our dads," Pepe Elías says.

"Your dad works in the *Presidencia*," I say. "And *pinche* Gordo, your dad works in the Treasury. What, your fathers' wages are a thousand bucks a month but they can afford to send their kids to the *Tec de Monterrey* at five grand a semester? How does that happen without someone getting ripped off? Just because my Old Man uses a gun and your

fathers use a pen doesn't make them any different."
In México, the guy with the most money is always
expected to pick up the tab, or else he's called "*a
muerto de hambre.*" Which I guess is the reason rich
and poor don't mingle too often in México.

I start to hunt out a new group of friends. I try
to sit next to the guys wearing sunglasses figuring
lente obscuro, mariguano seguro, but people aren't
too open about getting high in México. I end up
meeting my weed connection in Monterrey through
Poncho, the drunken brat my Old Man has me
rooming with. I'm standing in front of tía Gina's
house smoking a cigarette with Poncho and this
guy comes up to us and asks Poncho if he has seen
his brother, Blas. Poncho says he saw his brother
earlier and they're supposed to meet later, so the
guy keeps hanging around. Poncho has to go in to
take a shit or something, but before he does, he tells
me, "Watch this guy, he's a *pinche mariguano.* He's
probably just hanging around to steal something so
he can buy more *mota.*"

After Poncho leaves, I start making small talk
and learn that this guy is called Bam-bam by his
friends and that he doesn't study and is looking for a
way to go to the states to find work. Bam-bam begins
asking me all kinds of questions about the U.S.

"Are there any virgins in the United States?"
Bam-bam asks.

"There must be a few ugly girls out there."

"No," Bam-bam says and then makes a hole
with his fist and sticks his finger in like he's fucking
it. "I heard doctors stick their fingers up gringas'
pussies when they're born to rip them when they're
little so it doesn't hurt when they start fucking."

"I've never heard of anything like that going on."

"That's what I've heard," Bam-bam says. "That's
why they're so liberated and fuck guys like it's
nothing because they don't have a cherry to take
care of like Mexican girls do."

"I guess that makes sense."

"People make all kinds of money doing very little
work over on the other side, don't they?" Bam-bam
asks like it's something he's only looking to confirm.

"The salaries are better, but everything's much more expensive."

"But it's better than here, right? A guy can make some money and buy a car, maybe save some cash and come back to México and start a business."

"I guess a guy can do all that if he's careful, but like I said, everything's real expensive, rent, gas, food, electricity, everything costs more over there."

"Yeah, so maybe it will take some time, but at least I'll be making some cash."

"Sure, you can room with some other guys and not party too much and can save your money." I try telling people all the time that the U.S. is anything but the Promised Land, but you can't warn a Mexican about anything because they'll figure you're just trying to cheat him out of a good thing. Mexicans only trust what they see and oftentimes even doubt that.

"Not party too much, huh? That might be a problem," Bam-bam says.

"Alcohol and everything else is two, three times more expensive than here," I say. "Weed can get real expensive if you're up north."

Bam-bam turns to me with a start and says, "You smoke *mota*? The whole neighborhood's talking about Poncho's rich cousin from *el otro lado*, but no one said anything about you being a *mariguano*."

"Well, I've learned people don't look well on potheads down here."

"No, that's another reason I want to leave this fucking place. All these fools around here want to do is go to school and find a job they can do for the rest of their lives. No one gives any thought to expanding their mind or getting in touch with their soul with a little weed. It's just work, and save, and eat whatever meat is on special."

"If you know where to score for weed, I have a car and some cash. We can expand our minds till we're all kinds of fucked up if you want."

I start hanging around with Bam-bam and he introduces me to the local stoners. I learn all the places *mariguanos* go to share a joint—the tower by the alameda, the soccer field next to the architecture campus, the lookout over the *obispado*—and soon discover that I'm one of the few potheads who have their own car. This is important because these guys will do anything I ask—run to the store for cigarettes, score weed for me, sell weed for me, get me tacos, books, my laundry and anything and everything I need—just to slide behind the wheel of whatever car my Old Man let me take to school that week.

Comandante Torres never did give me that car he promised, but my Old Man changes my rides all the time because people are leaving him cars as gifts for favors and shit and this is another thing that freaks these guys out. People in Monterrey calculate everything they spend into interest. If a guy buys a car, folks start adding up the cost and maintenance and figuring how much that money would give back in interest if it was in a savings account. I guess this is why the people of Monterrey have a reputation for being *codos*, cheap. Since I change cars almost every other week, everyone has calculated my family to be "*archimillonarios*."

I keep trudging through school. The union for the *aduana* is able to get me in to a decent school but not the state-run university because my American diploma isn't considered sufficient preparation for university study. I wind up in a private school that is less strict on its entrance requirements. *El Centro de Estudios Universitarios* doesn't have the libraries, swimming pools, high tech labs, or hot shot PhDs that the *Universidad Autónoma de Nuevo León* has, but the classes are at night and most professors let you smoke in the classrooms, plus a lot of hot girls who fail out of the *Uní* end up here. Most of my professors work in state jobs by day and moonlight as instructors in the evening, so they've learned how to work both sides of the fence. They can recite entire civil and penal codes by memory and they stay up to date on every reform to *El Codigo Procesal*, but they also know exactly who and in what order to bribe officials to get a favorable verdict and still have enough money left over to make the case worth the trouble. Professors go over law books in class and how to give a *mordida* after class in bars.

Within a year, I'm moved into my own place and buying pot by the kilo and reselling it by the gram to the local stoners. My Old Man buys me a house in San Nicolas de los Garza so he can have a place to stash guns and meet with people while he's in Monterrey. He only comes into town every so often and when he does, it usually is just a stop on the way to Mexico City or Guadalajara or some other far-off point. These visits are brief enough for me to be able to sell dope out of the house without my Old Man catching on for a while, but soon the traffic in and out of the place gets to be so much that it's hard to keep people in line.

Selling pot to stoners is a hassle because everyone expects you to break out a joint and veg out for a while when you do the deal. Some stoners just hang around to mooch weed and see what they can steal, and I have guns and shit in this house. A few times, guys have tried to lift a piece I have lying around, and once my Old Man had to come down and slap guys around until the missing gun turned up. Bam-bam and the other guys I have running my errands try to take advantage of every opportunity to short change me, borrow my cars, take my records, hit me up for money, and steal whatever else they see. These guys act like they're entitled to all my shit because they know I move weed and besides, me saying no means I'm a "*muerto de hambre*" just like the guys from Reynosa say.

Even while I'm in Monterrey, my Old Man manages to call me every day to chew me out and send me to deliver a message or a gift to guys like the local *Ministerio Publico*, District Attorney. And he ends every instruction with, "And don't go over there all *chato*." I meet regularly with *comandantes* from different police corporations, *federales, judicial del estado, policía municipal, transito*—most times I am stoned out of my head—and all of these guys give me their cards. Anytime someone stops me on the street for a traffic violation or won't let me into a disco, I show one of these cards and I'm given the VIP treatment for the rest of the night.

When I meet with the *comandantes* and D.A.'s—
or *leyes*—I just tell them to call my dad if there's a
problem letting so and so out of jail. Then these guys
don't let me leave without taking me to a bar and
drinking the night away. I'm not much of a drinker,
but I stay up with these guys with a few hits of
coke, listening to the same old jokes or stories about
how they met my Old Man. These guys gush over
how grateful they are to my Old Man for teaching
them how to work and connecting them to the right
people. They always have a story about how they
were drinking with my Old Man and my dad got up
and kicked some tough shit cop's ass. I tell them we
do that every day when I'm home in Reynosa and
they think I'm a bad ass like my Old Man. *Leyes*
bully people, so it's important to let them know right
away that I'm not of the torturable classes anymore.

The codes and procedures I read about in
law school help me talk to the *leyes*, and I start to
understand just how big a favor they're doing by
letting some guy out who was caught with a gun
as opposed to a guy who was caught with a gram of
cocaine. It's not long before I get the hang of how the
system works and how money is made. When a guy
gets busted in México, for whatever crime, the first
thing the cops do is size up the fish they just caught.
If the criminal is a petty thief or some guy sniffing
glue in public, then it's a job for the municipal police.
Murderers, rapists, and violent thieves are jobs for
the *judicial del estado*, the state police. Anything like
drugs or guns is turned over to the *federales*. Once
the right cop has the unlucky bastard who's been
caught, they figure out just how much of a beating
they can get away with giving him. Cops have to
make sure the guys they slap around don't have an
influential uncle or *compadre* who can pull rank and
cause trouble down the line. This is the first chance
the detainee has to give a *mordida* or drop a name
and get his ass out of trouble.

Once the cops are certain who they've detained,
the *calientes*, beatings, start. Minor crimes like
public intoxication only merit a few backhands,

maybe a kick in the guts if the guy is drunk enough to fall. At this point, the drunk coughs up everything he's carrying and is released. More serious crimes get worse beatings. If the crime is against children or anyone helpless like a woman or the elderly, then the *judicial del estado* takes their time giving the *calentada*. There's usually no money for these crimes, but the *judicial del estado* makes up for the community service by shaking down thieves and pimps. The state police will always catch the crook but most of the stolen goods disappear.

Anyone caught with drugs or guns gets beaten until they tell where they scored. This is where the detainee should give up their stash and any cash they can lay their hands on, otherwise the *caliente* gets extended to another day and most likely won't get fixed at this stage anyway. The *comandante* of any police force decides how much and who can give a *mordida* and buy their way out of trouble. If whatever *bronca*, problem, can't be fixed with the *comandante*, then the *ministerio publico*, the D.A., gets his crack at a payday. While this is being decided, the detainee is still getting the shit kicked out of him. If the fix can't be agreed upon with the *comandante*, the D.A. piles up charges and threatens to return the criminal to the cops for further investigation until the guy crumbles and forks over a bundle of cash. The further up the judicial chain a prisoner travels, the harder it is for him to "*arreglar la bronca*," fix the problem. If the detainee can't fix the problem by the time he reaches the D.A.'s office, then he gets one last beating and is turned over to the judge, and lawyers get involved. Then all hope is lost.

It's a shitty system that plays on desperation. The more desperate a prisoner is, the more money a lawyer or someone who can fix the authorities can make. This is what I'll be doing for a living once I graduate. I figure I'll finish school and then marry Cynthia. Once I'm married, I'll run out all the stoners from my house in Monterrey. Cynthia will move in and I'll feed us by using the contacts I've made through my Old Man to get guys out of jail and make some cash. My plan's a good one, but then the phone rings.

"You need to come home right away," my mom says over the phone. "Your father's been arrested at the bridge."

"For what, who arrested him?"

"The police, stupid. Bring all the money you got. Your dad didn't even leave me money when he left. I don't know how I'm going to pay for this call."

"When did Dad get arrested?"

"Around ten this morning."

"He barely got arrested this morning and you're already worrying about who's going to pay the phone bill."

"Well somebody's got to think of these things, Johnny."

The main charge is conspiracy to transport firearms abroad. My Old Man and Onésimo are arrested at the international bridge in Hidalgo by the ATF just before they can cross back into México. The ATF has men staked out near the toll booths with a warrant for my Old Man's arrest charging the smuggling of five AK-47's out of the U.S. and into México. When the ATF rushes in with their guns drawn, my Old Man reaches for his gun out of habit, but he's unarmed and only manages to pull out one of the extra clips he keeps looped on his belt, which he throws at the ATF. The ATF adds assaulting a peace officer to the indictment. The ATF has him and Onésimo locked up in the federal holding cells in Brownsville.

There's a bail hearing. Onésimo is automatically denied bail because he's a Mexican citizen. The prosecutors argue that my Old Man's a flight risk because he has strong ties to México. The D.A. says that the gun shop owner—el dedo, the finger—will testify in court that my Old Man buys guns for people in México. My brothers and my sister and my mom are called to the stand and we tell the judge that we've never lived anywhere but in the U.S. all our lives. While on the stand, my mom manages to make friends with the judge and discovers they're related, although far removed. The judge sets bail at $100,000, and I have to hit up every *compadre* in my dad's address book to gather $10,000 to cover the 10% for the bondsman and another five grand for the lawyer.

The next day, I pick up my Old Man at the holding cells. I wait while the clerks pass me his belongings through a metal drawer that slides below the counter. The clerk tells him that he has to sign for his things before he can go. My Old Man acts like he doesn't speak English. I step up to the window and take the clipboard from the drawer. I show him where he has to sign. He signs the form and hands it back to me and says, "*Dásela a estos culeros.*"

"What'd he say?" one of the clerks asks through the hole in the window.

"He said, 'These guys are cool arrows,'" I say. "You know cool, as in good people, arrow like straight as an arrow. Cool arrow, it's the only English my father knows."

"I've never heard that before," the gringo clerk says. "Cool Arrow, that'd be a good name for my boat."

I take the wheel and start driving home to San Juan. My Old Man's going through his wallet checking cards and numbers he has written on slips of paper.

"None of this would have happened if you'd been home instead of *haciéndote pendejo* in Monterrey," my Old Man says.

"What'd I do? I didn't even know you guys were getting more *cuernos de chivos* for *Comandante* Goyo."

"My *compadre* Goyo isn't the only one who can have an AK. These were for me," my Old Man says. "If you'd have been around, you could've gone with Onésimo to talk to that *pinche* gringo at the gun shop instead of me."

"But then wouldn't I have gotten arrested?"

"It would have been your first offense. You'd of gotten off light," my Old Man says, then points for me to take a left.

"That way's the bridge," I say.

"I know," my Old Man says.

"The judge says you're not supposed to leave the country."

"*Que chinguen a su madre.*"

I pay the seventy-five cents for the toll at the bridge expecting ATF agents to come storming out at any second. We cross into México without notice. This is the last time my Old Man crosses the international bridge. A week later, I enroll in a law school in Reynosa, *La Universidad Mexico Americano del Norte.* I never even go back to Monterrey to pack up my clothes and belongings.

Chapter IX

After jumping bail on the gun charge, my Old Man moves my family permanently to Reynosa. We stay a few weeks at the Hotel El Camino, and then my mom and dad go out and buy a house. The house my Old Man, Mom, little brother Raulito, and I move in to in the El Parque subdivision is not a tract house like the one I had in Monterrey. The house in Monterrey was old and in a poor neighborhood and my Old Man was able to buy it for a little more than the price of a good used truck. The house in Reynosa is a residence, a thirty-eight million peso residence, in an exclusive neighborhood built for engineers who work for the *Comision Federal de Electricidad*, the light company.

Ours is the only two-story home on the block—hell, ours is the only fortress on the block. In front, on the left, there's a small balcony over the garage leading out from one of the bedrooms. The windows looking out from the two upstairs bedrooms to the street are rectangular slits a half meter high and two meters wide. The balcony and the upstairs windows thus provide perfect position and cover for shooting down into the street. The house is boxed in on either side and the rear by a three-meter brick fence with shards of glass encrusted into the top ring. There's no chance of being flanked by anyone trying to storm the house from the front because we install steel gates on either side to seal the gaps between the house and the brick fence. The front of the house is protected by a four-meter wrought iron gate. The only way into the house from the street is through the front door. There are long thin windows on either side of the front door filled with decorative glass. Anybody shooting from these windows can protect the front door for as long as the ammunition holds up, with plenty of cover from anyone shooting back.

The front yard is not very big, which reduces the kill zone beyond the main gate. This is why the upstairs windows and balcony are so important. If anyone can get past the iron gate, all the fighting will have to be done from the first floor. The front yard is small to make room for the huge back yard behind the house. There is a semi-Olympic three-meter deep swimming pool in our backyard. Next to the pool is a thatched roof *palapa* providing shade for a brick BBQ pit. The two bedrooms on the ground floor open up to the pool area through sliding glass doors. Each of the upstairs bedrooms has balconies the size of the lower rooms looking out over the pool. My Old Man seals off the gap between the two ground floor bedrooms by having a glass-encased dining area built that looks out to the pool. On top of the new dining area, my Old Man builds a TV room where we get the porn channels off the satellite dish. Behind the house and next to the pool is a dressing room and shower. In this room my father sets up his office and receives people to discuss business.

This is our new home, bought and paid for, and it's better than any place I ever stayed in the U.S. Suddenly, we're like royalty. Before Reagan and Bush restarted the war on drugs, everyone in town thought that traffickers were scumbags who poisoned children. Then, thanks to Reagan, the price of every drug that the U.S. is attacking goes up, and now everyone wants to become a cop or join a *clicka*. Pot, coke, Quaaludes, heroin, speed, everything is priced up three, four, five, times as much as you could get before the U.S. launched its newest plan to keep brown people poor. And the supply of drugs is on the rise because now guys move dope using the airstrips and roads the gringos made in Central America to aid some fuckers called the *Contras*. The price on the street keeps going up and up with each anti-drug commercial the U.S. puts out, while the price down south remains ridiculously cheap because of the volume of business they're doing. People are making connections to guys who buy shit by the tons. I hear names of places like Compton, Detroit, Atlanta, Boston, Brooklyn, and Kansas City from guys in the sierra whose main source of electricity comes from car batteries and gas generators.

Guys start to work together to make money off all the new markets opening up north by forming "*clickas*," kind of like social cliques, but with guns. Some guy goes north to work a construction site and meets a gringo stoner paying a hundred bucks for a quarter ounce of pot. These guys get to talking and figure they can make some money if they can get their hands on a few pounds of weed on a regular basis. The worker returns to México saying he knows a client in the U.S. who will buy a load of pot. Another guy has a *compadre* or brother-in-law who works in the *Federal* and can provide security for anything they move. These guys get together with another guy who drives a semi-rig and, through the cop friend, they make a connection with some grower in the sierra. All of a sudden these guys are trafficking drugs, moving money, and paying off the law. The newspapers and law enforcement call this organized crime. On the street we call it opportunity.

Of course, there's always the threat of someone trying to rob or shake down these *clickas*. Violence is a last resort in any business, but it happens, no matter if you're selling drugs or dresses. Dead bodies always make a mess of things. Some stupid motherfucker rips someone off and gets himself killed, then the next thing you know newspapers are splashing grisly pictures of bloated corpses on the front page and running editorials on the lack of law and order, getting the townspeople all riled up. Then the gossip chain and the finger pointing start and there're more bodies on the front page. Some do-gooder club like the church starts taking up a collection for the victim's family and public outrage grows into protestors in the streets shouting out names of crooked cops—all this fuss over a thieving son of a bitch who wasn't worth a shit alive. Then the cops have to pay off the reporters to keep their names out of the papers, which gives the *leyes* another excuse to shake down the usual suspects for a bigger *mordida*. And now no one wants to work because it's so hot, which stops the flow of cash. No one needs police poking around making business more expensive to operate or the townspeople out blocking up streets embarrassing us all, so a middle man, or what Beto calls a liaison, is needed to settle disputes between police and everyone working in trafficking. The guy who provides this service for any particular region is said to have *la plaza*. My Old Man has *la plaza* in Reynosa.

A lot needs settling by my Old Man. Issues like how much is fair for the *Federal* to charge a guy for wearing a gun around town while he readies a load for crossing. Or, should the state police be allowed to charge tax for a load passing through the town of Rio Bravo if the *Federal* has already been paid to ensure the load all the way to the river? This is the type of problem that comes up more often than people think. What do you do with a guy who *se baño*? *Un baño* or *bañarse*, like take a bath, means to rip someone off or to take more than your share in some deal. You can't just leave him lying in the street. These issues have to be settled through the guy who holds the *plaza*. Trafficking is called *la movida*, or now more recently *la maña*, because you always have something to move—drugs, money, weapons, people—and you have to be tricky about it. Every region the merchandise passes through on its way to the buyers up north in the States has to be *arreglado*, fixed, so the loads can get through without falling. Some guys try to work without *arreglando la plaza* by using ingenious *clavos*, secret compartments, and this is called *trabajando a la brava*. These guys only enjoy a few good runs before the law gets tipped off about a double floor on the trailer or that the pottery is loaded with pot. Then everything gets taken away from them and these guys have to go through whoever has *la plaza* to get their shit back. So basically, my Old Man is the guy people see when they need to pay off the cops whether it be before or after a crime is committed.

Guys from different *clickas* and law enforcement agencies come by the house every night. I make them check their guns at the door and tell them to take a seat on the wrap-around couch in the living room. Sometimes I have a *comandante* from the *Federal* sitting next to a drug runner from Michoacán, and these mortal enemies have to act like they're in Sunday school as long as they're under my Old Man's roof. Whether they be *leyes* or *mañosos*, they always slip me some cash, coke, weed, jewelry, bottles of cognac—whatever they think will get them to see my Old Man faster. I push the guys who bring me weed to the head of the line. I smoke the best *colas* that pass through Reynosa.

We have a full staff working the house now. During the day, my mom and a couple of maids run the kitchen and clean up the rest of the place. At night, the male staff comes on and we start receiving people for business. El Compadrito—we call him that because he has a habit of calling everybody "*compadrito*"—is a former waiter at La Majada, and he sees who wants a whiskey highball then scurries to the kitchen on his stubby legs to fetch the drinks. Polo is my Old Man's *compadre* from back in the days when we were living in Houston making collections for Don Ángel. Polo heard my Old Man is doing all right and came down looking for work. He used to peddle smack in Houston for Don Ángel. Now he's our cook. Beto screens our guests to see what business they have on hand then conferences over it with my Old Man in the back room. My Old Man decides what's fair for these guys to pay or receive for whatever they need fixed and Beto works out the details. Then my Old Man receives his guests "*no mas para saludar*" and everyone gets high for the rest of the night celebrating the deal.

We have more guys working for us. Even though everyone who comes to the house is looking for a favor and bearing gifts, swearing undying loyalty and all around gratitude just for an audience with my Old Man, we suddenly need a small army of bodyguards. I really don't see why we need all the extra guns. The traffickers just want to work and the cops just want to get paid, but my Old Man insists that *everyone* is out to get him. From all over México, he's recruited ex-cops and soldiers as his *pistoleros*. We have César from *La Huasteca Potosina* who used to be a state police officer in San Luis until he robbed the Aztec Money Exchange house in Monterrey. César is fair-skinned and can easily pass for an Irishman because of his thin red hair. César came with two other guys, Hernán and el Poca Voz. Hernán is in his twenties and has almond-shaped eyes that shrink to nothing when he gets high. When this happens, we call Hernán el *Vietnamés*. El Poca Voz talks in a whisper and is an ignorant son of a bitch. He's short, dark, and sports the thickest blackest hair I have ever seen. I gave César, Hernán, and el Poca Voz their AK-47's when they first came to work at the house, and el Poca Voz, like a *pendejo*, goes and chambers a bullet while my back is turned to him. If I had had a gun on me I would have shot him dead.

Panchito Martel is from *Tamazunchale* but I call the town Thomas and Charlie just to fuck with him. Panchito wears his pants low under his potbelly. His gut hangs out so much over his belt that it looks like he is on the verge of tipping over. He looks more like he should be selling fruit on the side of the road instead of guarding the front gate, but he can pull a gun and empty a clip into anything he points at faster than a transit cop can take a *mordida*.

Panchito was a cop in his hometown before he came to work for us, but he had to leave his job after he tortured some rich guy's son to death while trying to get a bigger *mordida*.

These guys are cool—except for el Poca Voz—and they always share any coke that they score or give me all the weed they can get their hands on, and each and every one of them swears that they will lay down their lives for me and my Old Man should any shit start. But of all the guys who work for my Old Man, Toño is the only one I trust enough to be my *pareja*, partner. One look at Toño and anyone can tell that he is a direct descendant of some barefoot Aztec warrior who ran through the jungle carrying fresh fish for Montezuma's lunch. Toño is from Mazatlan Sinaloa where he was in the Marines before being discharged for getting into a shootout over some whores with the *Federal* in the red light district. Toño smokes weed with me—the other guys just like to do coke and drink—and knows how to roll joints better than any *mariguano* I've ever met.

My Old Man takes these guys on the road with him when he travels to other *plazas*. Everywhere el *comandante* Torres del Rey gets transferred to, my Old Man goes in and sets up a meeting with the local drug dealers so they can figure out who is going to pay what to the Feds. Torres offers the same deal to everyone: they can pay a set price for seventy-two hours of *disimulo*—looking the other way and playing dumb in the office for three days. The *mañosos* move as much of their merchandise as they can out of the area during that time. After the three-day layoff is complete, all deals are done and any load being moved is fair game. My Old Man gets a cut of the action from the dealers and his *compadre* Torres.

Between semesters and holidays—México has a lot of holidays—I travel around with my Old Man and Beto to these meetings. I see México through a mirage of lakes, fountains, and seas stretching out in front of my windshield on the endless road. These aren't fun trips where we drink and sing love ballads like we did when we traveled to Los Ramones that time and stole all those sheep. On these trips we ride in a caravan of two or three cars filled with guys bug-eyed and lock-jawed from too much coke, toting AK-47's. Seldom do we talk about anything other than whether whoever we're about to meet might try something. Mostly we ride in silence with the occasional sound of the dropping of safeties on our guns when a car passes us on the highway.

I get to meet the guys who have the *plaza* in all kinds of different cities and towns in México. There are a lot of guys who have setups like el *Comandante* Goyo has in Durango, and a bunch of other guys who do work like my Old Man. I meet Jaime Espinoza, el Colorado, who is from Guadalajara and is the major buyer of all the pot grown in the sierra of Jalisco. I meet el *comandante* Villalón who heads the federal police in Uruapan, Michoacán. Villalón provides protection for the Villamontes family who control most of the pot and all of the cocaine that passes through the state. I meet el Toro de Oro, who runs the state of San Luis Potosí and who recommended César, Hernán, and el Poca Voz. I meet Don Celestino, who runs the biggest operation of all these guys. Don Celestino's territory is based in the state of Sinaloa but stretches all the way to Tijuana in the north and Jalisco in the south. He owns the Hotel Las Américas where we stayed that time with el *comandante* Torres and Don Gato and the rest. These guys run *clickas* down south, and they all need to be able to pass their merchandise up north. Working through Torres del Rey, we're providing safe passage for so many guys that we don't have to run loads of our own anymore. We get a cut from all the tons and tons of weed and cocaine the Feds let pass through their checkpoints, and every day there is a new *comandante* who wants to work and a new *mañoso* who wants to buy them off. Business is good.

Not everyone is happy with the new policies the U.S. is pushing on México. The guys from Mexican customs are starting to worry about a free trade agreement between the U.S., México, and Canada. This trade agreement, NAFTA, lifts the tariff on a lot of the stuff that used to be *falluca*, contraband: perfume, whiskey, frozen chicken, etc. The *aduanales* are seeing a drop in their *mordidas*. So many *aduanales* are ditching work and coming over to our house in their green uniforms that it looks like tryouts for Peter Pan are taking place in our living room.

First the agents working *la línea*, the line, come by complaining that all the *falluqueros* are demanding to pay less for their contraband. The agents say that the *contrabandistas* threaten to wait till the tariff is lifted to pass their goods if the *aduanales* don't cooperate. Then the *comandantes* from the *aduana* show up at our house along with their subordinates. The *comandantes* complain that the line agents are kicking up less *mordidas* on every shift. The line agents argue that they can't kick up more *mordidas* if the *falluqueros* refuse to pay. The *comandantes* are afraid they are going to be transferred to some place in the interior where there are no *falluqueros* to put the bite on if they don't keep up their payments to the directors and other higher-ups in the state department. We hear these guys cry all night, night after night, over how it's the end of the *aduana* and how they have been betrayed by their own government and sold out to the gringos. Then the head of the *Sindicato de la Aduana* comes by our house.

Carlos Ruiz Pequeño is the head of the Mexican Customs Workers Union, *el Sindicato National de la Aduana*. Ruiz Pequeño is the coked-up guy I met on our way back from Durango who helped me get into law school in Monterrey. When he shows up at our door, I escort him directly to see my Old Man and personally serve him his drinks for the rest of the night.

"It's the end of an era, Don Julio," Ruiz Pequeño says to my Old Man. He stares into his whiskey highball, swirling the drink around before taking a long pull. "But it could be the beginning of a better time for all of us if we could just manage to help get *un amigo* into *Los Pinos*."

"The Presidential elections are still a couple of years away," my Old Man says. "We won't know who'll be in charge till then. All my friends in the *Federal* and anyone else working for the government share your same worries, but what can we do? We just have to wait like always for who ever comes with their hand out after the elections, and then work will pick up again."

"I'm afraid it's not going to be like that this time around," Ruiz Pequeño says. "This new treaty with the gringos will cause the *aduana* to disappear and be replaced by *Hacienda*, the treasury department."

"Well, when that happens, we'll make some calls, find someone who knows someone else, and get you guys jobs with *Hacienda*," my Old Man says, then snaps his fingers and points to Ruiz Pequeño's glass so I can refill it.

"That won't help either," Beto says. Beto's sitting on a wingchair in the corner gnawing away at the skin around his finger nails. "The new trade agreement lifts the tariffs on so many goods that the only *mordidas* to collect will be for guns and ammunition, which of course cannot be legally imported."

My father turns to Ruiz Pequeño who nods and says, "It's the end of the *falluca* business forever, Don Julio. But it doesn't mean we're necessarily finished collecting *mordidas*. We can still make a living off of all the contraband traveling to South America, but we need a friend in *Los Pinos*."

Ruiz Pequeño wets his lips and looks around the room, stares at the door like he's expecting it to burst open, and then says, "I have some friends in Tampico who head up different workers unions. I have el Kino, the head of the *Petróleos Mexicanos Union*, willing to back us."

"Pemex?" My Old Man looks from Ruiz Pequeño to Beto, who nods his head *yes*.

"And we can get even more support, but it takes money," Ruiz Pequeño says. "Money and people win elections, Don Julio, and I believe there is no one better than you to help with this cause."

"I'll match whatever everyone else has to pay," my Old Man says.

"This is a little different than securing a *plaza*, Don Julio," Beto says. "Mr. Ruiz Pequeño would like for you to convince el *Comandante* Goyo in Durango, el Colorado in Jalisco, and especially Don Celestino in Sinaloa and the rest of the people in our line of work around the country to contribute to this cause. Then we can name whatever *comandante* we want to whatever region we want."

"Then, this would help my *compadre* Torres del Rey, right? We can get him named *Primer Comandante*?"

"Sure," Ruiz Pequeño says. "We can do all of that, but I thought you would prefer to be named *Primer Comandante* yourself, Don Julio."

"No, let my *compadre* Torres do it. He likes playing cop," my Old Man says. "But why should just the *mañosos* have to pay? I think the *comandantes* who want to keep working should kick something into the pot, too."

"You're absolutely right," Ruiz Pequeño says. "That was the second part of the plan. I was just about to bring that up."

"More than money, we still need votes if this plan is going to work," Beto says. The meat around his fingers is almost completely raw and he has to wrap a napkin around his finger tips before he can continue speaking. "We need for Don Celstino and the rest to convince their people in the sierra to vote for our candidate. With votes and funding from these gentlemen we can ensure at least six years of uninterrupted business for anyone who supports us."

"These men believe in you, Don Julio," Ruiz Pequeño says. "If you can get them to help us out, then I can promise that el Kino will get everyone who works in Petróleos and every other union in the Republic's vote. We'll have direct access to *Los Pinos*, Don Julio. We'll be rich."

"You're damn right these guys believe in me. I have my name and people have to respect it. I can get my *compadre* Torres and my *compadre* Celestino, el Colorado, and everyone else to back this plan as long as you can promise that we get to say what *comandante* goes where for the next six years," my Old Man says. He rises and shakes Ruiz Pequeño's hand.

I follow Beto into the bathroom and watch him run cool water over his tender fingers. Beto is smiling despite the fact that at least one of his finger nails has pried off.

"What's *Los Pinos*?" I ask.

"That's what the President's house is called in Mexico City," Beto says.

"And you guys are going to fix the elections so you can be in tight with the President," I say. "Isn't that a lot for us? I mean, we just barely got the *plaza*. Why not just keep on like this? God, you're talking about buying the President of a whole country! What, you think we're the Kennedys?"

"And when the new government gets in to power and your dad's *compadre* Torres is transferred to some desk, what are we going to do then?" Beto says.

"We can run our own loads again," I say. "Someone we know always gets named *comandante* sooner or later anyway, so what's the difference?"

"If this works out the way we've planned, Johnny, every *comandante* in the Republic will have to pay us a *mordida* along with all the *mañosos*," Beto says.

"We'll be like don Coroleone in *The Godfather.*"

Beto laughs. "This is going to be better than any movie. It's better than being any Godfather." Beto throws the towel over my head and starts to spin me around and says, "We're going to be rich."

I know we can do this. When I was a kid, a few years back, my Old Man helped this guy named Ramsey, who was this Chicano politician everyone was afraid was going to screw up the governor's race in Texas. He was taking votes away from this old guy named Clements. Clements's man—some guy named Karl—calls Ramsey and tells him they've put three tons of pot on his farm: Ramsey can either take the pot and throw the election or he can stay in the race and get busted for the pot. Either way there wasn't going to be a Mexican having a say about who was in the Governor's mansion in Texas. Ramsey called my Old Man and the pot disappeared almost as fast as his support at the ballot box. So if they could do that in Texas, we could step it up a notch and do it in México too.

We get out of the bathroom and go back to my Old Man's office. He and Beto start figuring out who they're going to call first. I tell el Compadrito to serve a round of highballs. There're more people who need to see my Old Man. I go back to checking guns at the door for a while then step out to smoke a joint with Toño. We stand on the curb in front of the house watching our guest sitting in the living room through the decorative glass.

Toño peels the foil paper off the wrapper around a pack of cigarettes. Once the foil is all off, Toño crumples the paper over and over until it is soft enough to use as rolling paper. This is called smoking "*en canal.*" A lot of *mariguanos* in México smoke like this because the cops will slap the shit out of anyone they catch with rolling papers. The joint tastes harsh and makes me cough for the first few tokes.

"You know, Toño, very soon we won't have to smoke *en canal* ever again," I say. "Soon things are going to get a whole lot better around here."

Toño takes the joint from me and inhales. He lets a little smoke drift out of his mouth then sucks it up through his nose and says, "There's nothing better than this."

I hear laughter from inside the house. My Old Man is in the living room whistling for el Compadrito to bring him a whiskey highball. He shakes hands with the men who have been waiting. Everyone is on their feet with a highball in their hand. Polo is in the kitchen beating avocados into guacamole. Panchito is standing by the door trying to adjust the strap on his AK-47. César, Hernán, and el Poca Voz are following my Old Man around the living room like shadows, AK-47-packing shadows. Everyone is smiling, drinking, laughing. *Banda* music starts to come over the stereo from the upstairs TV room. In a corner, all by himself, Beto sits gnawing away at the meat around his fingernails.

Chapter X

Everybody is doing something productive now that my Old Man has the *plaza* and a steady flow of money. My oldest brother, Chilo, is opening a nightclub in McAllen. Chilo plans to have live bands perform in the club. Real big name acts like La Mafia and Mazz, as well as new talents like that little *ruca* from Corpus named Selena who supposedly has the nicest ass in Texas, are all slated to feature at C City.

My sister, Lourdes, left her gringo boyfriend and is now doing the interior design for the club. She's shopping her ass off, buying up designer tablecloths, carpeting, lights—long fucking expensive racks of lights that move in waves to the beat of the music—velvet ropes, centerpieces, glasses, and bar equipment to make sure it will be a first rate night club, right down to gold-plated keys for the front door.

My other brother, Junior, is building some stables in Alamo to house all the horses my Old Man has been receiving as gifts. Junior does the shoeing, breaking, reigning, feeding, grooming, and hauling for my Old Man's horses. When Junior's not busy with our stock, he has to travel to different ranches in the U.S. and México to shoe our father's *compadre's* horses.

My brother, Rubén, has a deal with different car lots in Houston. The car dealers give Rubén cars they can't sell and he brings them down to the Valley before the dealerships report them stolen. From the Valley, Rubén and I cross the cars into Reynosa and I sell them to cops or to guys who work in the D.A.'s office—anyone with a badge can drive a hot car in México. Rubén likes to brag, especially about shit he knows nothing about, and is always getting himself fucked on deals. He brags about being able to get a grand for each car because that's what he hears a hot car is worth on all the cop shows on TV. Instead of charging his guy at the dealership for making the cars disappear, dumbass Rubén hands what should be his take over to his contact as if they were doing him a favor. I don't make a dime on the deals, but if I don't unload the cars for him he might get in hot water on his end for making promises he can't deliver. I don't say shit because he's older and has a family to feed, and I hate seeing him look like a *pendejo*. El Chaparro says brothers are supposed to look out for each other. And he's right. What kind of piece of shit wouldn't help his own brother?

Even my little brother, Raulito, is doing his part to adjust to the move to Reynosa. Every morning, Raulito drives his Z-28 Camaro across the international bridge to the ninth grade campus of PSJA on old 83. Raulito is only fourteen and looks every bit of twelve behind the wheel of the Camaro, but the Customs agents at the bridge can't even give him a ticket for driving without a license as long as he can show them his papers. After a few weeks, Raulito says the agents don't even bother to ask if he's an American citizen and just wave him through. U.S. customs agents are federal and have no jurisdiction over state laws, so a kid can drive a car across the border or someone can drive shit-faced drunk across the border and not hear a peep out of *la migra* as long as they can say "American citizen" and be convincing.

Yeah, everyone is doing something productive—with Dad's money.

At home, the guys who party with my Old Man show up and take off around the clock. It's not just *comandantes* or *aduanales* and traffickers hanging out at the house anymore. Now we have lawyers, doctors, engineers, journalist, editors from magazines, Senators, *Delegados*, and everyone else who calls himself a journalist or works for the government. Everybody wants to make sure they have a *hueso*—a bone, that's what they call government jobs—in the next administration. Word's out that my Old Man is going to be even more "*bien parado*" than he already is once the new *sexeño* begins, so people come by and kiss up to Don Julio. They ask for my Old Man to baptize their babies, be godfather at their daughter's wedding, come to their son's graduation—anything to build a bond, become a *compadre* to the man with all the *palancas*, leverage.

Partying hard is a Mexican's favorite way to get in good with someone. And this seems to work out fine for these guys because they're all incorrigible drunks who have discovered that cocaine allows a man to drown himself in drinks and not pass out. This is called "*tomando con truco.*" So many people come in and out of my house that I can only grab a few hours sleep here and there, mostly just little naps while sitting on the couch or a chair. I sleep in my clothes. On one of these days, I thought I had lucked out because, aside from the music and loud talk coming from the back room, the house is relatively quiet. It's noon and I'm lying in bed. I've only been asleep for a couple of hours after spending the night at La Majada waiting for Rubén to deliver some cars.

I feel a hand come down hard on my leg. I wake with a start, throwing punches at the air around me. The bed sheets start to slip out from under me and I'm rolled off the bed onto the floor. Before I can decide which way is up, I hear my

Old Man say, "Why is it always so hard for you to wake up?"

"I was asleep."

"But that's all you ever do."

"Sleep ain't all that bad. YOU should try it sometime."

"Maybe I would if I could get some help around here."

I'm about to point out that I'm on the job more than the paid help when I notice Beto picking up the spilled bed sheets and gathering up my boots. I shake my head to catch my snap and get myself off the floor. Memo Velasquez is standing in the doorway and I can hear the living room behind him filling with voices.

"Get yourself fixed up then come out here," my Old Man says leaving the room.

I take my boots from Beto and ask what's going on, but Beto just grins and follows Memo and my Dad into the living room.

El Compadrito, Polo, and el Chaparro are sitting around the breakfast table with their heads held in their palms. The *pistoleros* are alert as ever and standing at their posts; Toño is dozing, slumped over the counter, and el Poca Voz is leaning shut-eyed against the nearest wall. In the living room, a dozen men form a half circle facing me as I come out of the bedroom. These guys have been here all night and their clothes fit loose, their shirts are streaked with spilled whiskey, and more than a few have specks of piss sprinkled down their pant's leg. The rest of the group is made up of clean-shaven guys in cheap suits. My dad and this little *viejito* in a big suit are at the center of the group. The old guy has a face like a Volkswagen beetle with its doors open. His eyes bulge behind thick green tinted glasses that are held up by funnel-shaped ears. His nose is sharp but is lost by the enormity of his mouth. His features are so in contrast with his dainty frame that he looks more like a freak show midget dressed as a carnival barker than he does a federal judge.

My Old Man introduces him as el *Licenciado* Aruelio Mijares. His moldy lemon-colored skin is cold and clammy as he stretches my hand and says, "*Mucho gusto, joven,*" like the fuckin' grim reaper.

"El *Licenciado* Mijares is the new *Juez de Distrito,*" my Old Man says. "He's just in from Michoacán."

"Oh, *Licenciado,* it's a pleasure to meet you. I'm at your service for as long as you're in our town."

"I'll hold you to your word," Mijares says then lights a cigarette with the butt of his last cigarette. I take the butt out of Mijares's hand and smash it out in the nearest ash tray.

"Your father has given consent for you to come and work for me at the *Juzgado.* Now I know your father is rich enough for you to have no need of a job, but it is important for a young law student like yourself to be acquainted with the inner workings of the legal system." Mijares turns to the men on either side of him and says, "We must support the efforts of our young for they will someday be in our place." The suits and drunks snap to attention and nod solemnly.

I turn and look from my Dad, to Beto, then to Memo Velasquez and the rest of the men standing in my living room and they're all wagging their heads and smiling like some one just got tricked into fucking a transvestite.

"El *Licenciado* Mijares has something for you," my Old Man says.

Mijares finishes his cigarette then fumbles inside his suit pockets for a bit and pulls out an index card with the green, white, and red sash of the Mexican flag slashed diagonally across the front. "As an official employee of the Mexican Federal Government, you will need proper identification."

I take the card and read silently: "*Poder Judicial Federal.* Be it known to all authorities both civil and military that the bearer of this document is an employee of the Republic of México and entitled to all rights and considerations granted in the Constitution for the successful exercise of his duties." The card is filled out in my name with Mijares's signature in dark brown cursive scroll as the authorizing entity behind my appointment. When I finish reading and

look up, the men in the circle fall in around me. My
Old Man is the first to hug and congratulate me then
the others take turns, hugging me, patting me on the
back, and reminding me not to forget "*los pobres*."

El Compadrito, Chaparro, Polo, and the rest
of the guys snap awake and start refilling whiskey
glasses. Memo Velasquez and Beto take me off to
one side while the rest of the men in the room turn
to congratulate my Old Man for—shit, I guess for
raising me.

"What's going on," I ask holding up my new ID
card.

"You just got a *charola*," Memo says. "You've
got yourself a federal *hueso* to chew on."

"But what the hell am I supposed to do?"

"Learn to act like a lawyer," Beto says. "Take
money from people and do nothing in return."

"There're all kinds of ways to make money in a
court house, Johnny. And there are so many *viejas*
working in a court house that you won't have time
to fuck 'em all," Memo says, then he goes dark.
He pulls out a black 9mm Browning High-Power
from his waistband and holds it in the palms of his
hands. "This gun has killed five men. I wanted to
retire it after I shot it out with el Bigotes but I had to
find the right person to pass it on to." Memo hands
me his gun. I move the slide and see that there is a
bullet in the chamber. I push the safety up then slip
the gun into my waistband. Memo takes off his belt
and pulls off a leather case with two extra clips and
hands them over to me.

"That gun's never failed me, Johnny. I wouldn't
give it to you if I didn't have faith in it."

"Thanks a lot Memo, but are you sure you want
to give up such a thing?"

Memo holds up his palm and says, "No, you'll
be doing me a favor. Five is enough."

"I've got another gun for Memo," my Old Man
says. I hadn't even noticed he was standing next to
me when Memo was giving me the gun. "I always
said that the day one of my sons started wearing a
gun would be the last time I could ever get a night's

sleep. Don't give me cause for any more worry, you hear me? I don't want to know of you getting into any fights or showing off. That shit's for *pendejos*. Remember, guns are like women. Only real men can use them."

"I won't let you guys down."

"I won't let you guys down," my Old Man repeats after me. "Just embarrass me by letting yourself get caught smoking that *pinche yerba* while you're working at the court house *y me las vas a pagar*."

"I don't ever carry any *mota* on me other than in my head."

My Old Man steps in and grabs me by the arm. "That shit stops right now."

"El *Licenciado* Mijares would like to have a drink with both of you," Beto says poking his head between me and my Old Man.

Mijares chugs four more whiskey highballs and smokes a cigar before he declares lunchtime over and the cheap suits file out of the house. From the curb, I promise to report to the courthouse the next day at 9:00 o'clock. The living room is cleared by the time I make it back in the house but I can hear slurred conversations between hurried sniffs and exhaling sighs coming from the back room.

I corner el Poca Voz in the kitchen and pull out my new badge and press it against his forehead.

"*Poder Judicial Federal*, motherfucker." I dig into his breast pocket and pull out a hundred dollar bill folded in a coke pouch. I unfold the bill and do two big bumps off the end of a butter knife then pass it to Toño. I grab my keys and a beer for the road and head over to Cynthia's house to tell her about my new job.

Cynthia's thrilled over the news. She dances a *cumbia* around her sister's kitchen, shaking that beautiful ass of hers and swishing her boobs about like a stripper. She says we can get married in a year or two.

"Why in a year or later? Why not now or five years from now?"

"We can't get married now so soon after you got this job. Everyone will say I just married you because you got a good job. You want everyone to think I'm an *interesada*? And five years is too long to wait."

"Interested? In what? Who would think that you would marry me just because I got a chauffer's job?"

"It's with the *Federal* isn't it?"

"Yeah."

"Well, everyone knows that any job with the *Federal* is as good as a magic lamp."

"So you do want to marry me for my job."

Cynthia's eyes fill to the rim with tears. "Please don't say that." She wraps her arms around her chest and bends her head and begins to sob. I pull her into my arms.

"Hey, I was just kidding around. I didn't mean it."

Cynthia buries her head in my chest and says, "I've got something to tell you. I want you to hear it from me instead of someone else."

My face burns and my head fills with thoughts of Cynthia with another man and I want to pull my new 9mm and shoot her in the face.

"What did you do?" I ask hugging her closer.

"When we first started going out, I wasn't attracted to you."

"So you'd go out with other guys?"

Cynthia jerks her head up and nearly hits me on the chin in the process. "No, I'd never do something like that to you." The angry look goes out of her eyes and I can see a slight blush coming on. "It's just that I wasn't sure if I liked you for a boyfriend, but I still kept going out with you because I was bored and you always took me to nice places and bought me flowers and things."

"So it's all about me taking you out and spending money on you?"

"It was. In the beginning. But now I just care about you. I—you know."

"You what?"

"You know."

"Tell me then."

"You haven't told me."

"I love you, Cynthia. I've loved you ever since that first night I met you at the *Palenque*."

Cynthia looks up and presses her mouth to mine. We kiss long and hard and when we finish Cynthia sighs and says, "*Yo tambien.*"

"Really, Cynthia? You love me? You love me like that—like man and wife type of love? You love me enough to do—to do *eso*?"

"Well, when we're married we can do '*eso*' all we want."

"Really? Let's get married now."

"No. In a year or two. I don't even have to imagine what people will say if we get married now." We kiss again and my hard-on wants to break out of my Levi's. Cynthia doesn't move away like she usually does when I get this excited. She slips one of her legs between mine and grinds against me those parts of hers that means she's serious. When we stop kissing, Cynthia looks up and says, "I just hope I can hold out for another year."

I try to wrap her in my arms again but she bites me on the lip and pulls away.

"No, that's enough for now," she says holding me at arm's length.

"Oh, come on, just a little more."

"No, that's enough. Look at you, what if Linda comes out of her room?"

I look down to my pants and see the wet spot growing at the end of my hard on.

"Come back tomorrow and we'll make plans for our wedding."

I kiss Cynthia again and we finish with her biting my lower lip till she draws blood. The blood leaves a copper taste in my mouth, but it's worth it to hear her say that a year seems like an awful long time.

I got a job. My girl just told me she loved me. I want to do something to celebrate, but it doesn't seem right to go to the whorehouse. Besides it's a school night and I've got classes. I nose my Mustang toward the International bridge but instead of turning into one of the toll booths, I head south on Guerrero street. I skirt the *Zona Rosa* then turn left on Colón toward the *Central de Autobuses*. I take a right on Javier Mina and follow the street till it ends at the railroad tracks. I park my Mustang and cross the tracks on foot into the *vecindad* where el Pecas lives. This part of town is known as La Canta Ranas.

La Canta Ranas runs along the railroad tracks under el Puente Elevado up to la central de autobuses. The *colonia* is made up of cinderblock rooms that were abandoned when the red-light district moved to the edge of town at the end of Aldama Street. Squatters took over the cantinas and whorehouses and made *vecindades*. El Pecas lives in a complex where five families share a bathroom and a courtyard.

El Pecas's room is divided in two. There's a stove, refrigerator, a tin Corona table, and a few fold-out chairs in the back part of the room. In the other half of the room, through a sheet-covered doorway, is a double-sized bed. El Pecas was yanked out of this bed one night by the *Judicial del Estado*. The state police was investigating the murder of a guy who had been stabbed 17 times. A six-year-old witness placed el Pecas with the victim before he was found dead. The *Judicial* busted into el Pecas's room, blindfolded him, and loaded him up into a Suburban before he could even wake up. El Pecas says all he can remember is screaming "*¿Quién es? ¿Quién es?*" before the pain rained down and it went dark. The *Judicial* beat the shit out of him for three days before they realized they had the wrong guy. El Pecas has slept on the floor ever since that night. I sleep on this bed sometimes when I can get away from my house.

El Pecas works at a gasoline station on the corner of Colón and Bravo by day and studies law at the same school I go to by night. He scratches out a living by ripping people off at the pump. Every time someone pulls in for a fill-up, el Pecas works the pump to where it doesn't fully erase the last purchase. El Pecas pockets what ever he can scam at the pump, but it's a tired trick that more and more people are picking up on and he sometimes has trouble making enough to pay for tuition. I help him out by fronting him weed. El Pecas sells ten and twenty thousand peso 'tubos' of weed around La Canta Ranas, and we split the take.

I find el Pecas pacing up and down his kitchen with an open law book in one hand and a lit joint in the other. He's shirtless, showing the wiry frame of a bantamweight. He has light skin and reddish hair on his face and chest. The hair on his head is dark brown and he wears it slicked back and short around the ears.

"Johnny, Johnny, Johnny, have you studied, Johnny, have you studied?"

"I went over the chapter a few times last night at La Majada. I think I have it down."

"Why'd you study in a restaurant, Johnny? I thought you had to smoke *yerba* to study." El Pecas hands me the joint. "I have to smoke *yerba* to study, Johnny."

"So do I, but I had some time to kill." I take a few drags off the joint then fan the air with my new ID card from the *Juzgado*. "Hey, guess what? I got a new job." I hand the card over to el Pecas and let him read while I smoke.

"*Poder Judicial Federal*, Johnny, *Poder Judicial Federal.* You've made it to the big mafia now, Johnny."

I smile through a cloud of pot smoke.

"Your dad got you this job, Johnny? How'd you get the job, Johnny?"

"My Old Man called me into the living room and introduced me to the judge. I start work tomorrow."

"Yeah, yeah, yeah, your dad introduced you and you start tomorrow." El Pecas stops and thinks for a moment like *se le va la onda*. He has a habit of doing that. "Johnny, I have some money for you. A half a million pesos, Johnny. Remember Johnny, from that weed?" El Pecas goes into the other room and brings the money from under the mattress and starts counting it out on the table. "I've made it big too, Johnny. I'm paying off the *Federal.*"

"Hey, that's right," I say then finish off the joint. "I'm going to have to start taking more on our split now that I'm a *Feo*."

"*Sí, Sí, Sí,* that's what I was just thinking, Johnny. I was wondering if you were going to charge me more now."

We smoke another joint then head to class for our test. At school, the professor changes our exam to cover a different chapter from the one we were assigned. I end up having to fork over half the money el Pecas paid me to our Professor so that he doesn't fail us on this exam. El Pecas is mad about the exam. He doesn't like to pay for his grades and most times doesn't have to. El Pecas and I compete for grades, and he always beats me. If I get a seven, he gets an eight. If I get an eight, he gets a ten. I could give *mordidas* to all my professors and make better grades than him but then everyone will say I just bought my degree. Everyone says that anyway, but at least he and I know different. El Pecas wanted to file for a re-test, but I went ahead and gave the professor his bite for the both of us.

"You shouldn't have given him any money, Johnny." El Pecas slides low into the seat of my Mustang and covers his eyes with the palm of his hand. "You should've taken out your gun and threatened his life, Johnny. You're a *Federal* now, Johnny. You can get away with that kind of shit. I wish I could do that kind of shit. I'd show the *pinche ratas.*"

"They barely gave me the *charola* this morning," I say. "I can't go threatening people before I start work."

"It's nighttime already and you'll be working by tomorrow. You should've at least slapped him upside the head with your badge."

"Yeah, so everyone can think I got all *chiflado* because of my new job," I say nosing my Mustang through traffic. "I get enough shit about being a spoiled junior because of my Dad."

"I know you're not like that, Johnny. I know that you don't like to abuse what you got. I'm glad you're not like that. I wouldn't have started talking to you in class if I thought you were a spoiled junior." El Pecas lights a Raleigh. "I watched you for a long time before I started talking to you. I could tell right away you were a *mariguano*. Ray Ban trooper glasses even after it got dark, and the way you'd be all chatty like a parrot one day then all quiet the next. Once the whole class was at the snack bar and you were just standing there waiting for your turn, but the lady behind the counter asks you what you want first. Everyone just looked at you, Johnny. Do you remember that?"

I drive through the night traffic smoking a joint and tell Pecas I don't remember, but he keeps talking anyway.

"There were people ahead of you but the lady asked you what you wanted before everyone else. She could tell just by looking at you that you were *el bueno*. You looked around and saw everyone looking. I saw you do that, Johnny. You looked around then told the lady to give you an orange *Joya* and then you told her to give everyone in the class whatever they wanted. You handed the lady a twenty dollar bill and then just walked away with your soda. Everyone wanted to kiss up to you after that but you'd just go off and read by yourself like you always do."

"Those motherfuckers just want to sucker me for the tab. I'll put up when I have to, but I had enough of that bullshit when I studied in Monterrey."

"I know Johnny. I know people kiss up to you all the time because you have money. But you don't act like a rich guy. You don't humiliate people when you get the chance. I'm glad you're not like that. But sometimes, like tonight with that *pinche rata* professor, I wish you were like that."

"I'm not rich. I wish people would add up all we have to pay out to the Feds, *Judicial*, and now even senators and congressmen. And maybe everyone wouldn't think we're rolling around in money."

"Your Dad pays off the *leyes*, Johnny. The *Federal*, the *Judicial del Estado*, they all get a cut."

I take the joint from Pecas and say, "All those motherfuckers come by for their *mordida*. That *pinche* Rocha guy from Rio Bravo is at the house every Friday like it's payday or something."

"Senator Rocha from Rio Bravo."

"*Delegado* Rocha."

"*Sí, sí, sí, Delegado* Rocha from Rio Bravo, and senators—you said senators too—come by your house for money, Johnny."

"All the fucking time."

I turn away from Herón Ramírez street and head west along the canal toward my neighborhood. "I think the senators and congressmen get a cut for helping us buy a piece of the presidency."

"You guys are going to be able to pay off *Los Pinos*? Your Dad is going to have access to the President?"

"We get to name whatever *comandante* to whatever *plaza* we want as soon as the next President takes office."

"You guys are going to have all the *plazas*."

"Right."

"And you got a job with the *Federal* now and elections are still over a year away. *La tienes hecha,* Johnny."

"*Así es.*"

"You should've taken out your gun and threatened that professor's life, Johnny."

I pull my Mustang in front of my house and take a few more drags before I get off. I lean in through the driver's side window and tell Pecas to wait while I go in to get some more weed for him to sell. I don't think Pecas will ever try to rip anything off from my house like the guys in Monterrey did, and I've told him this, but he still refuses to come in. I go in the house and out the back door to the pool area. I grab a half kilo of weed I've got stashed under the BBQ pit and take it around the side of the house and slip it to Pecas between the bars. I go back in and tell my Old Man I'm going to give a friend a ride home. My Old Man makes me take Toño with me.

Toño rides in the back seat with an AK-47 standing between his knees. El Pecas is rolling a joint in the passenger's seat.

"Johnny, Johnny, Johnny, right now when we were at your house, I saw a guy."

"Which guy was it? What'd he look like?"

"Tall, skinny guy. Drives a Chevy Eurosport."

"That's Richard," Toño says from the back seat.

"Oh, him. That's just one of my Dad's godsons. He works for Don Celestino out of Sinaloa. He's been hanging around for a while now."

"He's from my neighborhood, Johnny."

"Well, he's moved up. Don Celestino loves him like a son and Don Celestino runs a big operation."

"He used to sell copper and scrap metal when he lived in my neighborhood."

"Well, like I said, he's moved up."

"*Dicen*, Johnny, I don't know, but they say Richard killed el Dr. Del Sol."

"The guy who used to own our school?"

"Yeah, yeah, yeah, they say the owner of the other law school in town paid Richard to drive up on a motorcycle and shoot el Dr. Del Sol."

"I remember that hit. The shooter walked up to the house and asked for the Doctor and shot him at the front door."

Everything Pecas was saying made sense. Richard talks like he's from Sinaloa right down to calling kids *plebes* and everyone *compa* and he listens to *banda* music. But I can tell he's originally from Reynosa. He knows that Balboa street is called *la linea del gas* because the gas line runs under it and that my neighborhood is called *la colonia de la luz*. These are things only a native of Reynosa knows.

Richard's been hanging around my house for the last couple of months. When people ask, he says he's on commission from Culiacán. Richard somehow made it to Sinaloa and got in good with Don Celestino. The engineer who owns the El Bravo College, the UMAN's academic rival, is from Sinaloa. A hit on someone like el Dr. Del Sol would have earned Richard an inside track to a new *plaza*. That explains how Richard got to Sinaloa but it doesn't tell me anything about what he's doing back in town.

Richard wears his Colt .38 in a Bianchi side holster with six extra clips strapped around his waist—a trick he picked up from my Old Man. The guys he rides with are decked out in similar rigs along with AK-47's. My Old Man's been lending him his Crown Victoria ever since Richard came into town. That's my Old Man's favorite car. All this time I thought Richard was some sort of cop.

The next day I wake up late for my first day of work. I gun my Mustang and before I can make it out of my neighborhood, I get stopped by a *transito*.

"*Lo siento amigo*, but I'm late for work," I say to the cop as I flash him my new badge. Before I can fish a few dollars out of my pocket to give him a *mordida*, he apologizes for stopping me.

"*Perdón, Licenciado*, it won't happen again," he stammers.

It takes me half a second to figure out what's going on then I say, "*Quítate a chingar tu madre.*"

Chapter XI

Judge Aurelio Mijares comes into office at the *Juzgado Sexto de Distrito* and immediately starts firing *licenciados*, secretaries, and anyone else he can and replaces them with some friend or relative from Michoacán. People at the *juzgado* say they resent me being hired because the guy who got fired from my job is married and has kids and doesn't come from a well-placed family like mine. That's what people say, but the real reason I'm not well-received is that they figure I'm some sort of spy for the judge. Everyone at the *juzgado* is worried about being next on the chopping block.

The judge doesn't need me for this type of dirty work. In his thirty plus years of working for the *Poder Judicial Federal*, Judge Aurelio Mijares has learned every dirty underhanded trick in the book to get someone fired or even prosecuted. His favorite dagger to stick in the back is hiding *expedientes*, legal files that contain all of the court proceedings for cases that fall under federal jurisdiction for our district. These files are kept in duplicate, one for the judge to study and another for the *Secretarios*, the lawyers heading any of the three penal *mesas* or *amparo*—writs—sections of the courthouse. The judge likes to come into the courthouse when only the night watchman's on duty and sneak an *expediente* out of some secretary's desk and then casually ask the *licenciado* to produce the file the next day so they can go over some legal point together. When the *licenciados* can't produce their copy of the *expediente*, the judge flies into a rage, places them under arrest, and threatens prosecution. By this point, most guys usually break and beg the judge to accept their immediate and irrevocable resignation. I see a lot of people's careers come to a screeching halt when some *expediente* "accidently" slips behind a bookshelf or gets lifted from a filing cabinet.

It takes me months to get my coworkers at the *juzgado* to stop with the sideways stares every time I come around. I run errands for the secretaries—there's a difference between secretary and *secretario*; secretaries are typist and *secretarios* are law clerks—going all over town for the best tortas and tacos for their midmorning breakfast. I give rides home to as many secretaries as I can cram into my Mustang everyday after work. I arrange the crossing of all kinds of household appliances for the *licenciados* who clerk under the judge. I do everything I can to get on everyone's good side. I even use my Old Man's contacts in U.S. customs to get border passing cards, *tarjetas local*, so my coworkers can cross into the U.S. and do their shopping. Not many people in México like gringos, but everyone loves to shop in McAllen.

I never have to drive the judge around because my Old Man hires an ex-waiter from La Majada for the judge's personal chauffer. I stay in the *juzgado* assigned to the "*oficialía de partes*" where I help a girl named Nancy receive all of the indictments, *amparos*, and motions filed by attorneys. It's my job to receive a document, stick it in a time clock to record the exact minute it was filed, stamp it with the federal seal of the *juzgado*, stamp it with a folio number, register the document in a big leather bound book, and then take it to its corresponding penal *mesa* or *amparo* secretary. The indictments go to any of three penal *mesas* that are in rotation, and any *amparo* against violations to Article 22 of the Constitution—illegal detainment and/or seizure of documents and property—is immediately turned over to the *primer secretario* because those have to be processed within twenty-four hours.

When work is slow, I steal off to one of the penal *mesas* or the *amparo* department and read *expedientes*. I learn that the only way to get off on a drug charge in México is to be charged with violating *Articulo 187 del Código Penal Federal*. This article states that if a person is a "*vicioso*," addict, and that the drug seized is intended for immediate consumption within seventy-two hours, then the detainee is eligible for bail and will be remitted to *el Centro de Salud* for treatment as opposed to being sent to prison. Being able to claim addiction is good to know because otherwise the Feds are going to charge that the drugs seized are part of a bigger shipment and the fucking *mordida* to get out of jail goes through the roof.

I also learn that there are all kinds of ways to bribe your way out of jail. The *comandante* is one level and has a price. The *mordidas* go up with the rank of the official taking the bribe. D.A.'s get bigger *mordidas* than *comandantes*, judges get bigger *mordidas* than D.A.'s, magistrates get bigger *mordidas* than judges, and Supreme Court Justices get the biggest *mordidas* of them all. But there're ways to get around having to go higher than a judge and paying a bigger *mordida*. A judge from a neighboring or higher jurisdiction can overrule another judge's ruling. In México, people can ask for protection against the police or a judge's ruling by filing for an *amparo* with the nearest federal judge. This is like a writ in the U.S. and can be used to stop a warrant or set a prisoner free if the federal judge says the lower judge didn't follow proper procedure. It's a slick get out of jail trick, but that doesn't mean that México's legal system is up for sale to anyone who has money, like in the states. There are certain things that are so unforgivable that no *mordida* can cover them.

One such case is the *narco-satánicos* who are kidnapping people and sacrificing them in satanic rituals out at El Rancho Santa Elena. These guys are running drugs across the border and making some pretty big scores, but instead of paying off the Feds, they drink human blood and butt-fuck on satanic alters so the devil will protect them. People start flooding the *comandante*'s office complaining about missing relatives and talking about how the guys out at Santa Elena are spending money like it's going out of style. But nothing gets done until a gringo kid goes missing. The kid's in Matamoros partying with a group of friends over spring break. According to the detainee's declaration, the *satánicos* see the kid break away from his friends to puke behind a parked car. The other partiers have only walked ahead a few steps when the *satánicos* jump out of their Suburban and grab the college kid.

The kid figures he's being busted for public intoxication because the *satánicos* are all decked out in police holsters and wearing caps with big PJF's patches, like regular cops. Halfway back to the ranch, the kid begins to catch his snap and starts to question why they're heading out of town. He knows something's up by this point and bails out of the Suburban and starts running toward the nearest car on the road, a Ram Charger. The guys in the Ram Charger flip on their sirens and jump out yelling "FREEZE." The kid figures he's safe now that the cops have shown up but it turns out to be just more members of the satanic ring. They load the kid back into the vehicle and take him to El Rancho Santa Elena. At the ranch, the *satánicos* bury him up to his waist, force a come-along wench around his spinal cord, and then tug the kid's spinal cord out, hacking at it with a machete as it rips out. He's still alive through most of this.

The ringleaders get nabbed in México City, but a few of the underlings get caught on El Rancho Santa Elena outside of Matamoros. These guys are turned over to the federal judge in Matamoros who dictates an *Auto Formal de Prisión* for drug trafficking. The *satánicos* file an *amparo* with our judge against the Matamoros judge's ruling. The *amparo* also asks for protection for a state judge's ruling on charges involving the kidnapping and murder of the American college student. Our judge denies that *amparo* and the killers end up getting raped during a prison riot in Matamoros.

From reading the *expedientes*, I also learn that almost everything we do at my house is illegal. Every time a group of guys gathers at my house, which is almost every night, and talks about bribing some *comandante* or moving a load of something, this is considered *asociación delictuosa* by Mexican law. Every load moved is considered a *delito contra la salud* and is covered by specific offenses like *trafico*, *posesión*, *distribución*, etc. Every guy carrying a fake badge is considered to be *usurpando funciones*. Every guy carrying a gun without authorization is guilty of *portación de arma prohibida*. Hell, just knowing about this stuff is considered *encubrimiento* and can land a guy in jail.

My coworkers are leery of me so I pick up on most of this stuff by reading or watching. Nancy is really nice to me though and good-looking with her pearly skin, short sandy brown hair, tits the size of orange halves, and round butt. She explains all the proceedings and what has to be filed where and why. Nancy is studying to be an accountant; most of the other secretaries are studying law so they can move up in ranks at the *juzgado*. I guess it's because Nancy's an accountant, and not a lawyer, she never figures out that since our department is the first to receive any document or motion, we're the first to know what's going on in every case that comes before the judge. We know when the indictments come and what detainees are coming in to declare without a lawyer. This is valuable information. Within a few months, I'm getting a thousand dollar *mordida* from lawyers for referring cases to them. I share my *mordidas* with Nancy by way of helping her set up a coffee shop and copy hut next to the *juzgado*. This business, El 6 ½, helps me out a lot because I'm forever having to leave the courthouse to go make copies for the litigants of the *expedientes*, which can take hours considering that most files are hundreds of pages of thick. I only get a *mordida* of twenty- or thirty-thousand pesos for this errand, so it's in my best interest to stay near the *juzgado* where my bribes are in U.S. dollars and a lot fatter.

Some cases are super fat. Miguel Porras escapes a medium security prison in Texas where he is serving time for laundering 750,000 undeclared and unexplainable dollars in cash only to get busted in Reynosa for smuggling two trailer loads of electronics a week later. Porras's face has been plastered all over the TV and newspapers on both sides of the river, and it's going to be hard for the judge to explain setting the guy free. But since it's not a drug case or high-profile killing, the fix can be set. Hell, the guy only evaded taxes. For a case like this, my Old Man has to step in and persuade the judge to find a legal loophole and pull off the *maroma*, flip. This type of case is worth hundreds of thousands of dollars because the guy made U.S. headlines, but little if any of that money ever trickles down to me or the *secretarios*—big case money trickles up, never down.

People start to notice my worth around the courthouse, and a year after trading in the chauffer's *charola* for an "*oficial judicial's*" appointment I'm given "*planta,*" which means I can never be fired. Right after that, I'm voted j*efe de sindicato* by my coworkers. I'm the union representative for the *juzgado* and every other federal judicial entity in our district.

Even though my Old Man leaves me out of the really big cases, which sucks because I'm bringing most of these cases to the table, I'm still pulling in a few thousand a week in *mordidas*. This income allows me to turn over my whole $660 a month pay check to Cynthia so she can finish paying on a fifteen-seat dining room set at Edelstein's in McAllen for when we get married.

I work from 9:00 to 3:00 and sometimes go back

in the evenings from 5:00 to 7:00. School starts at 7:00 and goes on till 10:00 at night. Between school, work, and sneaking off to see Cynthia, I have little time to be around the house. This isn't a big problem for me because I'm making money at the *juzgado* and I even get a chance to grab a couple of handfuls of weed from the evidence room pretty much at will. I want to bide my time in the *oficialía de partes* until I graduate and then make my run for a *secretario*'s appointment. And it looks like things might work out, until I get transferred to the "*Actuaria*." My new assignment has me running all over town to the different law enforcement agencies leaving notices that someone has filed an *amparo* against them or orders for the transferring of prisoners and other legal notices. I'm no longer in contact with litigating attorneys, and I'm away from the courthouse so much that I can't get in on shaking down any detainees. I complain to my Old Man, and he drops a big one down on me.

"I asked the judge to move you to a place where you couldn't get any *mordidas*."

"Why would you do that?"

"I also put the word out to all the lawyers that I don't want them giving you anything under the table."

"But that leaves me out of everything. How am I supposed to get by on what the courthouse pays me a month?"

"Damn it, I have a name. I can't have people knowing that my son is out hustling handouts. What'll people think about me? I can give you more money than you could ever make at the courthouse, anyway. If you need money, just come to me. But I don't want to hear about you hustling *mordidas* anymore, you understand?"

And just like that my wings are clipped at the *juzgado*. I shake it off by convincing myself that things will change once I graduate and get named *Secretario de Acuerdos*. I still have my *charola* for being the *jefe de sindicato* so I can blow off cops and get into places for free, and I can still make gas money copying *expedientes* so work isn't a total bust. By this time, most people at the *juzgado* like me despite my not being able to make more money for them. I get along so well with everyone at the *juzgado* that when my Old Man's birthday comes around, I invite the whole courthouse along with every litigant I know to the celebration.

The January before the July 1988 presidential elections, my Old Man throws himself the biggest and fanciest birthday party of all. These parties have been a big deal for the last few years—even before he got the *plaza*. And they aren't *carne asadas* like most people do for their birthday. My Old Man rents a hall and hires not one but several bands and celebrates for as long as he can go before passing out, which lately can take days thanks to all the cocaine. My Old Man's birthday is the social event of the year for all the *mañosos* in Reynosa, but this time it's also supposed to be a taste of how things are going to be after the elections.

The week of the party, the ladies hit the stores in McAllen and buy up all the evening gowns in La Plaza Mall. The cops' wives have to settle for off the rack Óscar de la Renta and Coco Chanell, but the *mañosos'* wives hit the specialty shops and snatch up the limited-edition designer dresses to make sure no other lady at the party is wearing the same dress. They know a little about designer names from magazines, but what they lack in fashion sense they make up in cash. "Are you sure this is the most expensive one you have and that there's not another one like it in the whole Valley?"

Later at the party, these ladies will start conversations by saying, "Can you believe this rag is all I could get for three-thousand dollars?" To which my mom replies with something that shows she's the *jefe's* wife, "Oh, I know, it's terrible. You can't find anything decent in McAllen. If more of you had papers, you could come with me to Dallas and shop at Neiman Marcus."

The men are worse than their wives when it

comes to their look. All of Reynosa's *mañosos* start making pilgrimages to *el otro lado* to have ostrich skin boots handmade at the same place Vice President Bush gets his boots, Rio's de Mercedes. Most guys hit Brittony's in the mall or Kalifa's Western Wear downtown and buy up the loudest silkiest shirts they can find. And everyone who's anyone is topped off with a 20X Stetson at five hundred dollars a pop. Even my Old Man's *pistoleros* wear suits and carry black compact HK-94 assault rifles that match their bolo ties.

The Reynosa airport is swarming with Lear jets. El *comandante* Torres del Rey and his *grupo especial* fly in on a confiscated jet from Mexico City. El Toro de Oro flies in from San Luis Potosí with his right hand man, Pompín, and a few pistoleros. El *Comandante* Goyo Fuentes flies in from Durango with Miss Nayarit on his arm and el Chano Godinez, el Güerro Gil, el Sapo, el Memo and ten other guys— all packing AK-47's. Everyone in the airport stops and stares as el *Comandante* Goyo and his men march across the tarmac with their AK's strapped across their backs and extra forty-round clips tucked into the waistbands of their Calvin Kleins. El *Comandante* Goyo stands in the middle of the airport lobby doing bumps out of a hundred dollar bill while his luggage is unloaded. Miss Nayarit, in tight jeans, western shirt tied in a knot showing off a firm abdomen, boobs pushing hard on pearl snaps, and a bottle of Hennessey XO cognac in her hand, casually smokes, then rolls her eyes and says, "What the fuck's wrong with all you *pendejos, nunca han visto un hombre rico?*"

Ramón *"el Clavillaso"* flies in from Guadalajara on his private jet with five of his men and four hundred *caguama* eggs—there's nothing better than sea turtle eggs to revive a man who is so coked up he can't swallow. El Quito comes in from Sinaloa with six hundred cases of Pacífico beer. Everybody brings something to liven up the party.

Guests bring their music with them from all over México. My Old Man gets his *compadre* Juan

Villarreal to play a few sets of Norteño music, then Los Líricos de Terhán hammer out some *cumbias* to get butts shaking on the dance floor. This is the local contribution to the party. After that, there's *Banda* music from Sinaloa, and the ladies all want to dance to that so they can practice doing "*la quebradita.*" The men are coked-up and gulping down whiskey highballs and don't care if they dance the soles off their new boots as long as they can run to the bathroom and do bumps off the tips of their car keys between songs. When everyone gets good and wired, the mariachis—the best Plaza Garibaldi has to offer—come on and play *Las Mañanitas* for *el festejado*. At the sound of the trumpets, My Old Man comes out of the bathroom like a runaway thoroughbred—*desbocanado*—going breakneck down the stretch, nostrils flaring, teeth bared, eyes wild and on fire, and skin gleaming with a light sheen of sweat. Flanked by César and Hernán, who stand with their HK-94's leveled waist-high, he takes the stage and stands under an arch of red, white, and green balloons dressed in a western-cut suit accented with embroidering down the lapels. My Old Man adjusts the gold clip on his bolo tie then doffs his beaver-skin Stetson at the guests while the flashbulbs go off. He looks immaculate. The women swoon and the men gasp in admiration. They call for a speech. A hush falls as my Old Man takes a deep breath and swallows hard. I can almost taste the coke lougy going down his throat before he says, "*Gracias, muchas gracias,*" through clenched teeth.

"Where there are men, *no hay fantasmas,*" he starts and the crowd hangs on to each word. "You all know me. You know if I say the horse is a roan, it's because I've got the hide in my hand. I've always tried to be a good husband, father, and friend. Good things are coming because I'm going to keep doing good things for my friends and family." The people huddled around the stage applaud. My Old Man holds his hands over his head until they're quiet again then orders everyone to "*diviértanse.*" He cues the mariachis to play on and wades through the guests feverishly shaking hands, stopping for more photos, getting pats on the back, then disappears back into the bathroom to do more cocaine.

Now that the mariachi is out, the guests take their turns belting out Vicente Fernández and José Alfredo Jiménez songs. Onésimo can sing so our *clicka* has a little representation, but almost every *jefe* has a guy in his crew who can really make the ladies swoon with their deep strong voices crooning promises to ride off with the damsel even if it means fighting to the death with the *hacendado*. Maybe *jefes* could stay in charge longer if they really listened to these *corridos*.

There are more local *conjuntos* always ready to take the stage so it's non-stop dancing for anyone who can keep up. And as if all this wasn't enough, there's this cool trio of guys from the Huasteca Potosina—where César, Panchito, Hernán "el *Vietnamés*", and a bunch more of my Old Man's *pistoleros* come from—going from table to table playing a violin, harp, and mandolin. They compose songs poking fun at the people listening, right there on the spot. *Para hablar de Julio Cortina, no se necesita buscar mucho. Don Julio le platica a todo el mundo y con mucho gusto, querreque.* It's amazing how they can call my Old Man a braggart like that and not get the shit beat out of them.

The music and dancing go on all evening till the sun comes up and long after that. The ladies are so happy to be dancing and talking about their expensive clothes that they don't try to wipe the coke off their husbands' noses like they did when the party started. The secretaries from the *juzgado* dance with the *pistoleros* from all the different *clickas*. The judge comes with his wife. He's more interested in drinking than dancing so his wife rips the floor with José Elizondo, one of my Old Man's *compadres*. After dancing a few songs with the judge's wife and her lifting her skirt way over her knee to dance a *zapateado*, Elizondo comes up to the judge's table and jams his Stetson down on the judge's head until it folds his enormous ears and says, "Here, at least look like a man."

I go into the bathroom, where my Old Man is standing in a ring of men passing a bag of coke around, and tell him that José Elizondo has just traded his Stetson for the judge's wife.

"The judge got a good deal," my Old Man says then turns back to address el *Comandante* Goyo, Torres del Rey, and Chuy el Tarta. "You see that's my point. Guys like the judge have a lot of power but they don't know how to use it. I have my name. That's all the power I need. And once the new President takes office, everyone will have to get in line."

I leave the bathroom and sit for a while with Roberto Pequeño, the head of the *Sindicato de Aduana*. I show him my new *charola* from the *Sindicato de Trabajadores del Poder Judicial Federal*.

"We're going to do great things," he says.

"They haven't even announced the candidate for el PRI yet." I've been following the news and know that the opposition has already named as their candidate an ex-governor from Michoacán and the son of an ex-president, but the PRI candidate is still being disputed.

"That's all taken care of, Johnny. Next week the PRI will reveal their candidate and all we have to do is wait for the inauguration then start filling suitcases with money."

"We still need Don Otoniel to be fingered for the candidacy, right?" I've heard Beto and my Old Man talking about a guy named Otoniel Camacho who is supposed to take office and pad the ranks of the federal police in our favor.

Pequeño lights a cigarette, holding the lighter to the tip long after it had lighted and sending a flame up high enough to scorch the cowlick hanging off his brow. "Don Otoniel? Yeah, don't worry, we've got that all taken care. As long as the PRI wins we're going to do great for at least the next six years."

In México, there's really no mystery as to who is going to be president once the PRI announces its candidate: they've won every major election since The Revolution. It's a well-known scam. The other parties yell fraud and then manage to land a government job anyway. Everyone gets a license to steal, and the PRI keeps on winning. Now they're going to use drug money to finance an election. The only surprise is that they hadn't thought of this sooner.

We've been handing over shit-loads of cash to PRI campaign organizers through Pequeño and his *sindicato* by securing transport for 700 kilos of Venezuelan coke. The Venezuelans are paying $3,000 a kilo on each shipment through México and across the Río Bravo and are running loads every two weeks. That's over two million for each load, and most and sometimes all of that money is going toward the campaign through the union leaders. And we aren't the only guys throwing down cash. Similar payoffs are collected and distributed from Don Celestino in Sinaloa, el Colorado in Guadalajara, el Toro de Oro in San Luis, el *Comandante* Goyo in Durango, and a bunch of other *jefes* from all over México. This election is already decided and we're paying for it.

Cynthia motions from across the dance floor for me to come sit next to her, so I leave Pequeño. We dance a few songs. Cynthia loves the party.

"I've never seen so many beautiful dresses," she says. "Are we going to have parties like this when we get married?"

"I haven't had a birthday party since I was five."

"I'll throw you birthday parties every year—you'll have to give me money—and we'll invite all of your dad's friends. Can I have a party for my birthday?" Cynthia's eyes are dancing faster than her hips.

"We'll throw you parties," I say and she gives me a peck on the lips.

"Oohh, we can have a party on my birthday and say it's for both of us since mine is just a couple of weeks before yours."

I sit her down with her sisters while I go outside to smoke a joint with Toño. I'm leaning on a car in the parking lot when Richard pulls up in my Old Man's Crown Victoria followed by a blue Suburban carrying four guys. I can see the barrels of their AK's poking up between the seats of the Suburban.

El Richard pours out of the Crown Victoria

wearing a Colt .45 with gold Mexican eagles encrusted on the grips mounted in a leather holster. He hands me the keys and says, "Here's your dad's car. Tell him I'm taking care of some business and that I'll be back later."

"You don't want to go in and party with us for a while?"

"Is Beto in there? I got 600 kilos of *mota* in Tampico that Beto's supposed to help me move. It's going to waste and fucking Beto hasn't lifted a finger. He's lucky he's got your dad to hide behind, but I swear if I ever get the chance I'm putting a bullet in his head," el Richard says.

"Beto's probably just busy with the campaign and getting things ready for after the elections."

"That's what I'm doing. I'm cleaning up this town so people will respect Don Celestino and your dad. There has to be respect. Without respect there's nothing. Beto's not showing any respect."

"I guess it's that extra bullet in the back of the head that gets all the respect, huh?"

"Some guys *no entienden con una sola bala.*"

"Beto's all right. I'll try to talk to him and see what the hold up is on your load. But you know how the *Viejo* is; I can't cut a fart without getting my Old Man's permission."

My joint's out, but before I can strike a match, el Richard steps forward with a light. He holds the flame steady and lets me fill my lungs with smoke before putting it out.

"We're the new generation, *mi Johnny.* You should come to work with me."

"I work for my Old Man," I say exhaling slowly.

"Sooner or later you're going to have go it alone, Johnny. We could make a lot of money together. You know all of your father's contacts and I can get merchandise directly from Colombia. We won't be mules for anyone anymore. People will respect us. We'd run the show."

"It's my Old man's show. He says how we run it and so far it's worked out for everyone."

"Your dad would still do his thing, but we'd

branch out and run everything else. We'd tax everyone who runs shit through our territory and not just the guys who work *arreglados*, like our *jefes* do. We can start taxing numbers, whores, liquor, everything. Even hotdog vendors will have to pay us if they want to work in Reynosa," el Richard says.

"Sounds like you want to take over the *Federal*'s job."

"Those fucking *putos* need to be put in their place. They take an oath to respect the law and here they are shaking us down. If I get my way, when this deal goes through we're going to start charging *them* to work. I'm telling you *mi Johnny*, we can take this *clicka* and turn it into a cartel."

"Oh man, cartel, you mean like they got in Colombia?"

"The new generation, *mi Johnny*," Richard says. "It's going to happen, just you wait and see, and your dad is going to be right on top and so can we if you say the word."

"It's something to think about but not tonight. Tonight's for partying," I say. "Are you sure you don't want to go in for a while? How 'bout a hit off this *toque*? It'll make you have sweet dreams."

Richard looks at me cock-eyed and says, "I light candles to keep from having nightmares."

He gets into the front seat of the Suburban and snaps his fingers. The vehicle pulls out of the parking lot and glides down the street dodging potholes like a shark swimming over a reef.

I go back inside and make a stop by el Chano Godinez and the rest of the *pistoleros* at *comandante* Goyo's table. Beto's sitting between el Chano and el Güero Gil and both men are leaning in to hear what Beto has to say over the music. El Chano gets up when I come up to the table. Chairs scoot over so I can squeeze in, but just then Beto gets up and leaves me his seat. He goes around and shakes hands goodbye, which is not unusual. But when he makes his way back around to where Chano and Gil are sitting, he leans in and whispers something in Chano's ear that makes Chano send me a sideways look. It's only a flicker of the eye, but I'm sure that whatever it is that Beto and el *Comandante* Goyo's men are talking about, they don't want me to overhear it. Beto leaves and crosses the dance floor over to my father's table, gnawing on his fingernails every step of the way.

The party lasts all weekend. My Old Man receives two Ram Chargers, a Marquis, a Ford Bronco, a Silverado, a Chrysler Fifth Avenue, a Dodge Prospector pick-up, three Rolex watches, Mexican Centenarios (hundred peso gold pieces), and a whole bunch of other expensive gifts for his birthday. My brothers, Rubén and Junior, get the Ram Chargers. Mom gets the Fifth Avenue. My sister, Lourdes, gets the Silverado. Raulito gets the Prospector. My Old Man keeps the Marquis and jewelry for himself, and I get to keep my Old Man's Crown Victoria.

Chapter XII

My Old Man parties for nine days after his birthday. Night after night, he just keeps drinking and doing coke with whomever shows up at the house. Most visitors leave after a night or two, but there's always someone showing up just as someone else is leaving. And my Old Man keeps right on gulping and snorting without missing a beat. He's like a kid at a slumber party, afraid to go to sleep before anyone else so as not to miss anything cool.

For the last couple of days of this binge, my Old Man speaks nothing but *babosadas. Comandantes,* traffickers, and other fools who drop by the house looking for a free high get cornered by my Old Man and are forced to hear violent accounts of *"gente que no vale madre."* The people he refers to are mostly backstabbing friends and double-dealers, but I hear my name and most of my family's names come up during my Old Man's rants. Guys nod or shake their heads trying desperately to follow along with the conversation only to be turned on and attacked.

"*Pinche Beto, no vale madre.*"

"That's right, Don Julio. *Pinche* Beto's a smart ass *hijo de su chingada madre.*"

"That's my right-hand man you just insulted, *culero*."

The *pistoleros* all know to spring to action and whisk away anyone who comes under the gun, but more than a few guys leave with busted lips and cracked skulls. It's pretty funny for a while.

On the ninth day, I wake up to find my Old Man propped in the corner of the back room, his .38 Super in one hand and an open pocket knife in the other. By this time, my Old Man can't speak a word. His jaws are locked from too much coke, *en trincado*. Anyone who goes within arm's reach gets jabbed at with the knife or swatted at with the .38. I don't think he has sense enough to drop the safety and actually shoot anyone, but I'm not sure. For hours, me, César, Toño, and el Chaparro take turns taunting my Old Man like we're going to rush him— to keep him from doing more coke. Finally, when he starts to nod off, el Chaparro and I are each able to grab an arm and take the gun and knife away. My Old Man slides down the wall and passes out before his ass touches the carpet.

We get him in bed and call el Dr. Reyes over and he runs an IV. Dr. Reyes shoots some liquid Rohypnol into the IV and leaves an extra vial with instructions to shoot a quarter syringe full every time it looks like my Old Man might be coming around. We do this for two days and nights. After that we just let him sleep on his own. A day later, my Old man wakes up, takes a piss, eats some fruit, drinks a half gallon of water then goes back to sleep for another day. My Mom keeps charge of the IV and calls out for us to help her when she takes him to the bathroom.

The *pistoleros* and the house staff lounge around the downstairs like it's a hospital waiting room. My sister, brothers, and their families come over from the other side and accept condolences and assurances from my Old Man's crew that everything is going to be okay. Everyone takes a seat on the couch and whispers diagnoses and speculates on recovery time like my Old Man has just come out of an operation or something. I get scowls and screwed up expressions whenever I remind the room that our dad is laid up because he made a pig of himself with all that booze and coke.

"He's a worse *mariguano* than I am," I say.

"Shut up Johnny, Dad's sick. He hasn't even sent me any money for my rent," my sister says. "He's never been late with that. It's got to be something really bad for him to forget *me* like that."

"He's got a Colombian cold. You should've stuck around all those nights after the party and jumped between him and the key of coke he kept digging into."

"That's enough, Johnny. Don't be talking shit while Dad's sick or I'll kick your ass," my brother Rubén says.

"Try it and I'll shoot you in the leg, motherfucker."

Rubén starts to square off on me and Junior says, "*Ya, párenle a su pedo.* I've got horses that need feed and you *pendejos* want to start more shit so I'll never make it upstairs to get some money from Dad."

My brothers and sister don't have a clue about anything that's going on around the house. They don't even watch the primary results on ECO when the news about the PRI candidate is sounded.

The PRI announces their candidate on the last day of my Old Man's bender and it isn't Otoniel Camacho. The nomination has gone to some bald fucker with a bushy mustache named Salinas. He looks like the guy from the Monopoly game except without the hat. Beto calls to check on how my Old Man is doing and seems unconcerned when I ask him about the switch.

"As long as the PRI wins, our deal goes through, Johnny."

"But I thought we wanted that Camacho guy?"

"We decided that presidential power might go to Camacho's head a little too much. Salinas will work more to our best interest."

"So my Old Man knows all about this?"

"What? Your father's been informed of every step. Now, I have some things to do. I'll call later to see about Don Julio. Let him sleep. It's best that he rest for now."

Even over the phone I can tell Beto's gnawing at his fingernails.

It's Sunday and Cynthia has gone shopping in McAllen with her sisters. No one at the house cares that a hangover is stalling the biggest deal we've ever been in on. I roll half a dozen joints and ride with Toño over to el Pecas's house. There's a game of soccer being played by a couple dozen kids in the street in front of Pecas's place. This kid, el Conejo, runs up to my window while the players clear the pile of rocks acting as goal posts so my car can pass.

"Pecas doesn't have any *mota*," Conejo says. A group of kids begins to swarm around el Conejo in a mass of mud-colored arms and bare chests, stretching their necks and elbowing their way up front to look into the car or streak their fingers through the fine coat of dust every car in Reynosa sports.

"Who said I was looking for *mota*?" I say pulling away from the flock of kids gathered.

Pecas's back door is half open. I jump into the kitchen pulling my gun and leveling it at the room.

"*Judicial Federal*, motherfucker."

Pecas turns from the stove with a pan of scrambled eggs and a spatula in each hand and a joint dangling between his lips. "*Pinche* Johnny, why do you have to come in getting me all *acalambrado*?"

"What you doing that you shouldn't be?"

"I'm smoking this *toque*. That's enough to get me slapped around."

I plop into a chair and throw a sandwich bag filled with joints on the table next to my gun.

"Let's eat," Pecas says going around the table scooping out scrambled eggs and chorizo onto plastic plates.

Pecas shuts the back door, but not before looking around the courtyard to see who's around.

"Johnny, I'm not going to sell *mota* anymore."

"¿*Qué onda*, you going to live off the coins you hustle at the gas station?" I ask then light another joint so that we each have one going. "You must've done something to be *asustado*."

"Don't worry about anything, *hay esquina*. El Conejo's out there and Omar; they'll get to us soon enough if any *leyes* start to come down on the *colonia*."

"Any fucking cops come down here, I'll flash 'em my badge and send 'em running home to their mamas."

"No Johnny, this shit's different." Pecas begins clearing the table, stacking the dishes in a tub and stashing the weed in a tin can he throws behind the stove. "There're these different guys, a commando. They came into the *colonia* a couple of days ago and busted Tavo Hasso. The *Feo* came right up to Tavo's house like he was there for a buy. Tavo said, 'Do you want *mota* or *coca*?' The *Feo* rubbed his hand across his mouth then backhanded Tavo. The other *Feos* rushed in and loaded Tavo up into a Suburban and took him to the *Federal*."

"They took him all the way to the *escuela*?"

"Yeah, to the *Federal*."

The *Policía Judicial Federal* had moved its headquarters from near the Bravo del Valle law campus to a school building that had been built next to the Valle de la Paz Cemetery on the outskirts of town, so now the place is known as *la escuela*, the school, where people learn the last lesson of drug dealing: you're only as good as your last deal.

"They got Tavo and a bunch of other guys from downtown, La Juárez. Even some guys from La Chicho over by where you live got pinched. They take 'em all to separate classrooms and kick the shit out of 'em."

"How do you know all this?"

"Ah Johnny, the *raza*. You know how we are. *La raza* is always in on all the latest. El Kangaroo has a *tía* who's dating the guard who opens and closes the gate for the *Feos* at *la escuela*. He saw them bring Tavo in and el Güerro Chiplee, el David.

Remember David, you bought that bag of really good *mota* from him, *puro veneno*, Johnny, remember? ¿*Puro veneno*? Well, all those guys *y chingos de raza maz*. They took them to *la escuela*, Johnny. *Dicen que gritaban bien gacho*."

"Don't worry, they're just getting the small timers. It's just a show." This is the first I've heard of this. "It's just another operative or some shit like that. They'll come in and take a few *bateadores* like Tavo to el D.F. just to show off for the newspapers then leave."

My Old Man only fixes things for guys moving big loads, but the small time pushers have to fend for themselves. This usually isn't a problem since it's the municipal police who patrol the *barrios*—they can be bought off cheap. But every now and then, the Feds run a raid on a few operators and things get hot on the streets. I guess that's what's happening now.

"The *Feos* are getting all the *bateadores*. All the guys dealing shit in Reynosa are either hiding or they've been picked up. They're up there in the classrooms, screaming their heads off, *bien gacho*, Johnny. Why are they picking up all the street dealers Johnny?" Pecas gets up and cracks the door and peeps out then opens and closes the door a few times fanning the smoke out of the kitchen. "*No hay pedo. Hay esquina, hay esquina.*"

"Who the fuck are these guys again?"

We had been talking in a stoner's stupor, each of us drifting in and out of the conversation haphazardly when Toño says, "It's Guillermo Gomez Culeroni. He was named *comandante Anti-aéreos* and he's stationed here in Reynosa now."

"Anti-aerial *comandante*?" I haven't heard of that title before, but that's not what bothers me. Why wasn't this new *comandante* at my Old Man's party?

"Your Dad's *compadre* Domingo Gonzálo told us all about the operative right after the party," Toño says.

"When was this?"

"After the party, at the house, your dad's *compadre* Gonzálo came around and said Gomez

Culeroni was coming and that he was going to be picking up all kinds of people. I was standing right behind your dad when he said it."

"So my Old Man knows this guy?"

"He's from here, Johnny. Gomez Culeroni is from Reynosa," Pecas says. Pecas goes around the kitchen, getting on tiptoes to scan the top of the fridge, moving everything around the table until he has searched the whole kitchen high and low and then comes to a stop in the center of the room. "He's from here, Johnny. I had the paper. Who took it? I saved it." Pecas disappears behind the bed sheet covering the entrance to the only other room in the house and comes back seconds later holding a newspaper. "Here he is, Johnny."

I read the article under the title, *"Hijo de Reynosa regresa a tomar puesto."* It doesn't impress me as anything other than your standard *There's a New Thief in Town* piece. "This guy'll come around the house soon enough; they all do sooner or later."

"This Culeroni guy *le vale madre.* He's coming with special orders, *caiga quien caiga.*"

"Special orders from who?"

"From somebody in México City, Johnny, orders from el D.F., that's what the paper said. Didn't you read it?"

"The newspapers always say that the *leyes* are acting on orders from México City."

Toño gets the newspaper and studies the picture over the article. Gomez Culeroni is standing next to a police helicopter wearing a striped shirt tucked into beltless pants like the kind Beto wears. He has his hand on his waist and you can see a pinky ring and a gaudy watch. A medallion hangs around his neck, probably of la *Virgen.* Except for the police helicopter and beltless pants, Culeroni looks like a *narco traficante.*

"He's got a big head," Toño says.

"He dresses like a fag," I say.

"Kangaroo's *tía* said that one of the agents told Culeroni that a *detenido* knew him and that he wanted to *arreglar.* Culeroni dragged the *detenido* out of the Suburban and pulled him by his hair all around the parking lot—in front of everybody, *chingos de raza*—kicking and scraping the guy all over the pavement. Then Culeroni stood on top of the *detenido*, stood right on top of the guy and said, '*Ya saben que a mi me gustan calientes.* I don't have any ties to anyone,' just like that, Johnny, '*me gustan calientes,*' standing right on top of the guy who said he knew him."

"My Old Man or someone we know has to know this guy."

"Your dad's *compadre* Gonzálo knows him," Toño says.

"See there, if Gonzálo knows him, then this guy must know Franklin, Severo Benavides, los Arredondos, all those guys. My Old Man is in tight with everyone right now." Gonzálo, Franklin, and all those other guys weren't at the party either.

"Culeroni's good friends with Franklin. Gonzálo said that to your dad that night," Toño says.

"Ramón Franklin, Johnny? Is that who you're talking about?"

"Yeah, his sister lives in our neighborhood."

"He was chief of the state police here in Reynosa," Pecas says. "He was in charge when they picked me up for that murder. '*Lo siento joven, Ud. No tiene nada que ver en esto,*' that's what he said when they were leading me out. Three days they beat the shit out of me and '*Lo siento joven*' is all he says. And now he's coming back."

Toño's bent over the picture of Culeroni again and every now and then he gets up and holds the newspaper at different angles to the bare bulb hanging from the ceiling.

"There must be some way to fuck these guys," I say. "The judge only looks at the confessions and is blind to the bruises. People just can't torture people and nothing happens." Fuck, this is what our crew is supposed to be around for; we have the *plaza*.

Toño holds the newspaper up to the bare bulb one last time then gets the cherry real hot on the end of a joint and burns a hole through Culeroni's face in the picture. He blows smoke over the hole and the edges begin to glow and spread till half the head is missing—for all I know, Toño might've just cast a spell on Culeroni. The paper falls to the ground and Pecas springs out of his chair and starts ripping it into pieces and gathering them in a neat ball he stuffs into the tin can that had once held all the joints.

"Your dad's going to do some deal with Franklin. Gonzálo said his sister is selling her house on the street over from your place. I think your dad is going to buy it," Toño says.

"There, you see, Pecas? My Old Man's got it wired." Well, at least he's wired, I think to myself. I tell Pecas we have to go. He doesn't let us leave until we help check the whole kitchen for anything incriminating we may have left behind. Pecas stands in the doorway as Toño and I cross the courtyard, his eyes all squinted up from the sun and says, "You have to write it yourself."

"*¿Qué cosa?*"

"Your declaration. You have to write it yourself. *Apenas así*, if you want to tell your side of it."

"You think?"

"*Digo yo, quién sabe.*"

"How the fuck would you know where to start?"

"*Allí 'ta el pedo.*"

"*Allí está el pedo.*"

El Conejo gets up from the bumper of my car as I walk up. He has his shirt hung over his shoulder and is still breathing hard from the soccer game.

"Who's winning?"

"This car came by a minute ago, Johnny" Conejo says. "It stopped by your car for a while then drove off."

"What kind of car?"

"A blue Marquis with no license plates. Probably *Feos*. They didn't look like state police either."

"No plates? Yeah, that sounds like the *Federal*. What'd they do by my car?"

"They just looked at it," Conejo says. "They gonna pick you up too?"

"Hell no," I say flashing my *charola*. "I work for the *Poder Judicial Federal*."

"You're lucky."

When Toño and I get back to the house, my Old Man is sitting at the kitchen table eating some soup.

"And the Lord said to Lazarus, *levántate y anda* and Lazarus got up and *ando*," I say.

"*Anduvo, pendejo,*" my Old Man says.

"Yeah, but only for a few days *y luego se le quito.* How you feeling? Ready for another one?"

"Another what? I collapsed from exhaustion. Every *hijo de su chingada madre* and their brother coming by and you don't do shit but send them right in."

I know the drill. My Old Man's got a "*cruda moral,*" a moral hangover. He feels guilty for making a pig of himself and acting all crazy, so now he's going to find something I did to piss him off and start jumping my ass. Usually all he needs for an excuse is to say I'm high, and most times he's dead on, but that doesn't change any of the other shit that's going on while he's waving his gun around at people. It's just like all those times before we had the *plaza* and we were waiting for loads. I could count the hours and tell how things were going. If the driver didn't report by a certain time, I knew the load was lost. I always got myself in trouble by asking my Old Man, "Shouldn't we've heard something by now?" And that was enough to send my Dad into a rage. I never have learned to quit asking the obvious.

"If you see that I'm getting tired, you could use your head a little."

"That's when you get the most mad."

"I have reason to be mad. Nothing ever goes like it should. My *compadre* Goyo got in a shootout with the soldiers in Durango."

Comandante Goyo had the whole state of Durango in his pocket. He had a federal *charola* signed by the *Procurador General de la República.* We're supposed to be months away from having the *plaza* at a national level, and now one of the main guys gets killed.

"They shot him in the leg and let him bleed out without taking him to the hospital or anything.

El Chano and el Güerro Gil have teamed up and are going to war with Don Celestino over who gets to keep control of el *Bisonte*," my Old Man says.

"What's Don Celestino got to do with that ranch? Chano and Gil were the ones running it with *Comandante* Goyo. Shouldn't they get to keep it?"

"*Pendejo*, my *compadre* Celestino and my *compadre* Goyo were partners in that ranch. How's my *compadre* Celestino going to look if he just lets those two take it?"

"Can't you go in and fix it like you did in Veracruz or something?" I'm starting to wonder if lines are the only thing my Dad can fix now.

"I can't do shit till the *cambio de poder* takes place. Why's that so hard for everyone to understand?"

"This doesn't seem right, Dad. I just found out a new *comandante* is in town and Goyo getting killed and el Chano and Gil. And did you know that Camacho guy didn't get fingered for the candidacy? Why wasn't this Culeroni guy at your party, Dad?"

"*Ya, cállate el hocico.* You have no idea how much shit I have in my head. You think I need to get opinions from a *pinche mariguano* like you? Just shut the fuck up for once. You walk in here your eyes all squinted up like a *pinche* constipated *Chino* thinking I don't know what you're up to while I'm busting my ass hanging on to the *pinche plaza.*"

"I was just asking."

"I was just asking. *Hazte pendejo.*"

He's pissed. He's yelling at me but he's mad because he can't answer my questions. He's feeling burned but desperately wants to disbelieve his instincts at the same time. I go into my bathroom and start to clean up but am jerked out before I can finish washing my face. My Old Man has me by the back of my hair holding me bent over, leading me out of the bathroom. I back away when we clear the door, and just out of reflex I grab the grips of my gun.

"What you hitting on me for?"

He squares off and takes a half step forward, but balks when he sees my hand on my gun. "You've got *pinche mota* stashed in the BBQ pit."

I see el Poca Voz standing behind my Old Man, smiling like a snitch.

"*Hazte pendejo*. There's a fucking operative going on and you bring that shit into my house? You bring that shit in here and it's me who takes the fall. You ever stop to think about that? You're going to ruin this deal for me with that *pinche mota*, you stupid *mariguano*."

I skirt my way around my Dad and pull my gun and smash it into el Poca Voz's face and it splits like a melon. I'm out the front door but can still hear my Old Man yelling, "*No vales madre*."

A few days later, I'm told to meet Beto at a notary's office—I have no idea what I'm lending my name to this time.

The notary, a small dainty little thing dressed in a suit that looks like it's halfway through with swallowing him down, coughs from behind a rustic-wood desk. He opens two leatherbound portfolios and sets them before me and Beto. I look over the one closest to me and see my name.

"I sign at the bottom?"

The notary stands over the document and points. "There and initial here then one more signature, there."

"Whose house did I just sign for?"

"Your father bought this house from Franklin's sister so he can have an in with Culeroni," Beto says. "I suggested it might be time for you to move to your own place, especially if you're going to be pistol whipping his *pistoleros*."

"You heard about that?"

"He wanted to make sure this got done before he leaves for Celaya."

"My Old Man's going to Celaya? What the fuck's in Celaya except for caramel candy and goat cheese?"

The notary's pacing nervously behind his desk. Every now and then he stops and inches the portfolio closer to Beto so he can sign it.

"Your father's going to stay there till after the elections. Don Gato bought a tire shop in Celaya and your father's going to stay near by."

"Don Gato left the *Federal?*"

"Yes. So did Torres del Rey, and Memo and Polo. Armando is the only one from the *comandante's grupo especial* still active."

"Why'd those guys quit? We're just about to move these guys anywhere we want, and they up and quit? None of this shit seems right, Beto. We're supposed to get the *plaza* for the whole nation but nothing looks right."

"It won't be official for a few months, but we thought it would be best for them to resign then come in again after the new President takes power."

Nothing makes sense anymore. Why would Beto think it's a good idea for my Dad's most loyal friends to leave their jobs just when we were about to take over?

The notary coughs again and Beto signs the papers and hands them back.

"We'll be finished in a moment," Beto says to the notary. "Why don't you go file those papers?"

"But I have to lock up. My secretary isn't in. I can't just leave without locking up."

"Then go wait in your lobby," I say. I shut the door behind the notary and go around the desk and sit in his chair. "Nosey motherfucker, that one there. So, all those guys left the *Federal* and that's supposed to be cool? What about our deal with those guys from Venezuela? How we gonna protect their loads without *comandante* Torres del Rey?"

"We can afford to suspend that operation for now. But even that'll be considered small-time compared to what we'll be capable of once the *cambio de poder* takes place. From now on, no more secret compartments to move our loads or paying off every checkpoint. Soon, real soon, thanks to NAFTA and this deal, we'll be transporting our goods with government seals to protect our merchandise."

"And if it doesn't go down like that, Beto?"

"Don't worry about these things, Johnny. I have it all under control. We'll get you something where you can give that little girl you're seeing a good life. You're serious about her, right?"

"Yeah, but I'm a long way from getting married. I've got some money saved up, over forty grand. But my Old Man cut off my *mordidas* from the *juzgado* and my friend Pecas doesn't want to sell anymore weed. I have to stretch what I got for now I guess."

"You're young, with a pretty girlfriend, you're about to become a *licenciado*, you have a good job. Why do you want to go around making your dad even tenser by putting doubts in his head? You have a deed in your hand. You should be showing off your new house to your girlfriend instead of worrying over nothing. C'mon Johnny, think about yourself for once."

Beto's being nice—in fact, *se esta pasando de bueno*, and he's basically saying trust me. Every day of my life has taught me to know better, but what if he's right? What if this is finally our big score? Maybe I can go it alone now.

I make it back to my Old Man's house just as it's getting dark. Don Chuy, our night watchman, is sitting in a Bronco parked in front of the house.

"They all left," he says.

"Who's they?"

"Your brothers, sister, their families, everyone."

"So, just my Old Man and the regulars are here?"

"No, they left too. Your mom, dad, all the workers, all gone."

"No shit, my mom and dad already left?"

I go in and find Toño sitting at the breakfast table cleaning a colt .45.

"Your Dad left for Celaya. He said he'll call later and for you to stay close to the phone."

"Where's everyone else?"

"Polo, el Chaparro, and the maids went home right after your father left. César, el Poca Voz, Santos, and his brother are riding with your dad. Your dad gave me what was left of the kilo after the party, but he told me not to give you any. You want some?"

"We'll half it up later."

I go from empty room to empty room. For the first time since we bought the house, I am alone. I'm the only one to say what's what around the house. No one to boss me around. No one to slap me around. I have the *plaza*.

I stand in the open doorway and call out to Don Chuy, "Hey, pull one of the trucks around front and help me load up my bed. I'm going to go smoke a joint in my new house."

Chapter XIII

I take the steps leading up to the *Juzgado de Distrito* two by two. The gun tucked in the breast pocket of my leather jacket bounces off my chest. The cocked hammer slams in just above my left nipple with each step. It hurts. I stop at the double-glass doors and shift the stack of legal files I'm holding from my right to my left arm. This is just an excuse to look over my shoulder again.

The red Chevy Suburban that has been following me all morning is pulling up to the curb opposite the courthouse. Through the tinted windows I can make out two silhouettes riding in the back seat. I lean into the glass door and the 9 digs deeper into the ripe spot on my tit. It's the only comfort I've felt all day.

The sweat on my palms chills as the air-conditioning hits me. I cross the dank corridor to the *Actuario's* station and give the files and the signed receipts for motions to *Licenciada* Tina. She mauls the stack with contempt complaining that I take too long to make my rounds. She forgets to thank me for doing her job. I light a cigarette and

lean strategically on the counter behind the painted
black eagles on the glass door so that I'm out of view
of the Suburban idling across the street. I lower the
zipper on my jacket and pull the grips of my 9mm
so the hammer clears the pocket and I go outside
again.

From atop the steps of the *juzgado*, I can see
into the Suburban. The driver is asleep with his
arms folded over the steering wheel. The passenger
in the front is facing me, curled up in his seat with
his back toward the driver. The shadow of a head
leaning on the tinted window tells me it is safe to
assume the scene isn't too different in the back seat.

Even if I take the time to pump two shots into
the occupants of the front seat, I can still shoot
whoever's closest in the back seat. That leaves only
one potentially active gun in the back seat. Or maybe
two. I might not have made a fifth passenger riding
back there. Maybe, if I only put one shot into the
guys sitting in the front seat . . .

Licenciados Chapa and Palacios climb the steps
of the *juzgado* to where I'm standing. Chapa is my
maestro from law school. He is very tall, which is
unusual because everything else about him screams
indio, right down to the thick black hair and dark
skin. Palacios is a scrawny lush known in legal circles
as a coyote attorney, a lawyer whose rare judicial
successes come from fixing cases. They're both my
neighbors. Chapa lives on the opposite end of my
block. Palacios lives on the next street over, behind
my father's house. The only difference between
Chapa, a litigator, and Palacios, a coyote, is that
Chapa will milk a client a little longer before putting
in the fix. Their faces are lit up like they've just met
a whore who takes IOU's. They want something from
me. I smoke and stare into the Suburban.

"¿*Cómo estás mi Johnny Juan*?" Chapa throws
his arms around me in a hug and uses the occasion
to pat me down to see if I'm packing a gun. "I once
asked the class what no retroactivity meant in penal
matters and Johnny Juan, in only his first semester
of classes, said, '*es cuando la ley no te puede chingar
de reversa para atrás.*'"

Chapa tells the same story every time he sees me.

Palacios pumps my hand. "That was pretty smart, Johnny."

Chapa stands between me and Palacios with his arms draped over our shoulders. "Oh, I knew he was smart from that moment on." Chapa hugs my shoulder tighter. "That must've been when you first came from *el otro lado*. I said right then and there, this is a good boy, even if he's a *Johnny Juan pocho*."

"I was just barely learning how you guys talk down here."

Palacios stands bent under the weight of Chapa's arm, nodding his approval. "You were right though, no retroactivity. They can't come back and fuck you."

"I told you he's smart." Chapa interrogates Palacios. "When we were driving over to the court house, what did you hear me say about Johnny?"

"You said Johnny's smart." Palacios follows Chapa's lead which means they've been rehearsing.

"Where's your father, Johnny?"

"On tour." The guy riding shotgun in the Suburban stretches then digs himself back into the seat.

"Ha, of course he is. He won't be back soon?"

"Not unless you know something I don't."

My Old Man left town six months ago. So did every other *mañoso*. My job at the *juzgado* kept me from leaving along with the rest. The new President hasn't named a *Primer Comandante* so no one knows who to pay. My Old Man and his *compadres* paid for the election but I don't think they got their money's worth.

Chapa follows my gaze to the Suburban and asks, "Are they here to leave a *consignación*?"

"I can't imagine why else they'd be here." I have to wet my lips to say it.

"Good, an indictment, maybe we can pick up some clients." Chapa runs a hand through his thick hair. "*Anda la cosa muy jodida.* I haven't had a new case fall my way in over a month."

"No one can move until the new *Comanche* gets named," I say. All the local operators are out of town waiting to see which *comandante* will end up overseeing the *plaza*. Until then, it's every man for himself for anyone stupid enough to stay. Every guy who can carry a badge claims they're in charge and tries to put the bite on. There've even been shootouts between cops over who gets to shake some poor fucker down. Drug dealers face the same problem as the police. Just as there are too many dealers for the police to catch, there are too many cops for the dealers to bribe. Violence in this business is never about turf or routes like the newspapers say; it's always over who gets to pay for protection from cops and other thieves. As in the U.S., there can be no organized crime in México without corrupt authorities. Right now, we live in a lawless town, and I'm standing in front of an empty *juzgado* as proof.

"There's still no word on when the new *comandante* will be named?" Chapa asks.

"I know it hasn't happened yet. I'd of seen or at least heard by now if the judge had received the notification from the *Procurduría*."

"And in the meantime, everything is locked tighter than a *señorita*'s knees. We haven't had a client with money fall for weeks."

"I hear there are over a 120 new agents and *madrinas* in town," Palacios says.

"What do you say, Johnny?" Chapa asks. "Are there more Feds on patrol?"

"There seems to be a lot more Suburbans without license plates on the road." I try to sound casual. "*La raza* can't score enough weed to mix a remedy for rheumatism."

"I hear this is a real bloodthirsty group that hit Reynosa." Chapa looks down on the Suburban and shakes his head. "They've got everyone lying so low, we can't even get a drunk out of jail."

"They do this every time they change *comandantes*." Palacios screws his finger into his clenched fist. "The big shots in el D.F. send up squads of agents to *chingar* everyone, then the new *comandante* gets here and sets a high quota and no one says a peep about it, just as long as there's work."

We move to let a lawyer and his client's family make their way out of the *juzgado*. I know the lawyer. He's green, with no connections inside the courthouse, so his case is stonewalled. He's having a hard time explaining to an older man and a woman carrying a baby why their loved one is still in jail despite the advance they paid months ago.

"Yes, Palacios, but it's the *madrinas* who are the real danger." Chapa waits for the passing lawyer and the disgruntled family to carry their squabble down the steps. "These pseudo agents are not accountable for any abuse they commit because they're sponsored by the Feds. I've heard that these *madrinas* the Feds brought into town are a lot more sadistic than your typical crew of *maleantes*."

The woman carrying the baby is standing on the curb yelling "*pinche rata*" into the passenger window while the older man she's with tries to keep the lawyer from closing his car door by holding tight to the handle. The attorney pulls away from the curb and the man's forced to let go of the door when he can no longer keep up with the accelerating vehicle.

Chapa cocks his thumb at the scene and shrugs. "I've heard of tortures far worse than your usual mineral water and pepper sprayed up a detainee's nose or cattle prods being put to the testicles, *hasta se meten con la familia*. I hear tell of the abuse of women and children, bludgeoning beyond recognition, *desaparecidos*, and even men being raped."

Palacios raises his hands in exasperation. "Imagine that, being raped after getting beat half to death."

"I can't imagine being raped any other way." I feel a slow chill, a purely physical sense of danger, a warning in my blood that violence, a shocking death, and torture wait for me impatiently. I've heard stories similar to Chapa's from the detainees brought before the judge. The detainees give their *declaraciones* barely able to stand—most pass out before they finish their testimonies. Their lawyers argue that the confessions were coerced, and the judge says, "That's what they all say." Then the detainee's really fucked, *reo que se confiese, que lo defiende su chingada madre.*

"Ha, of course you can't imagine getting raped without a fight." Chapa turns to Palacios. "When the police practice delinquency, we thank God for real men like Johnny's father." Chapa points his chin toward the Suburban. "Your father would never take any shit from usurpers like those parked across the street."

"And you're like your dad, Johnny," Palacios says. "*Hijo de tigre nace pintito.*"

I nod, wishing I was out of town like my Old Man.

Chapa turns his back to the street and cocks his head over his shoulder. "Just look at that bunch parked over there. They're asleep, probably tired from robbing people all night."

"They get to do what they please while honest men like your father have to leave town."

Chapa turns to stare Palacios down. "Out negotiating the safety of practically the whole town, I'm sure. That brings me to something that should be of great concern to all of us here present." Chapa places his hand on my shoulder. "Johnny, you know I'm the first to say that we all sleep better in our homes since you and your father moved into the neighborhood."

"*Gracias, maestro.*" When we first moved in, my Old Man made me take the crew on a sweep of the neighborhood. We slapped around a few guys who said they were just cutting through to get to their jobs and wrecked some stereos that were playing too loud and that quieted things around the *colonia.*

"And I mean that. Before you moved in, no house was safe from thieves."

"Yeah, yeah, and the police would only come for gas money to continue the investigation," Palacios adds. "Robbed twice."

"That's right. And that's why we don't want to go to the *judicial del estado* for that business about Don Lupe's lions, unless it's all right with you."

Guadalupe Benavides is the reason my father bought his house in El Parque. Lupín, as I call him, was a big operator back in the 70s, but he got pinched and doesn't do anything but occasionally warehouse loads on his property. He's got a big spread, enclosed by a nine-foot brick fence where a tanker trailer can easily be parked without being seen from the street. His friends are always giving him ridiculous gifts like 500 live quails, peacocks, toucans. Along with the birds, Lupe Benavides has 70 goats, a pair of geese, a spider monkey named Lady, a six-point buck, and three African lions penned up on the two acres where his home sits.

When I first moved into the neighborhood, Lupín sent a currier over to fetch me—he never uses his own phone for speaking with *la gente*. He sat me down at his kitchen table and fed me fried rattlesnake—he said it was good against cholesterol—and explained how my father was in charge of the neighborhood now, but he was still keeping active as "*sub-comandante.*" I was to function as *jefe de grupo* and report to my father as usual. But I also have to see to whatever Lupín might not be able to handle on his own. Now that both my father and Lupín are out of town, I oversee both outfits.

"I had Poncho and Gordo pen the lions up when Lupín left on vacation like I was told." And I haven't been back to check in on Lupín's place since. "Did they get loose?"

"No, the lions are penned." Chapa looks to either side then leans in. "They haven't been fed in ten days."

"I'll just buy a dead horse at the slaughterhouse." I've known Lupín's lions to eat half a horse every other day between the three. But a whole horse isn't going to satisfy the cats very much after a ten-day fast.

"Oh no, Johnny, that won't be necessary." Palaicos straightens to deliver his news. "I spoke with Don Lupe last night. He phoned me from his vacation site in *Ciudad Valles*. We discussed the lions at great length and decided the best thing would be for them to be killed."

This won't be hard to confirm, although I have no reason to doubt what Palacios says is true. Men like Lupe Benavides order hits like white men order Chinese food.

"You don't have to be telling the world where the *Señor* takes his vacation," I say just to take Palacios down a notch.

"With things being the way they are and the Feds riled," Chapa cups my shoulder like a horny priest, "we figured you'd rather we find *un agente del estado* to do the deed, so we can spare you any trouble you might not be able to handle."

I square off on both men. "Why'd you come to me?"

"You're *lugarten*—"

Chapa steps forward, quieting Palacios before he can call me *lugarteniente*, the term the media is using to describe the guy left in charge while the bosses are on the lam. "You're looking after Don Lupe's place while he is out of town aren't you?"

"Lupín's house and the rest of El Parque." I alternate glares between the men standing before me. "Do either of you have a complaint with how I've been handling things?"

"*No, no, no, para nada.*"

"*Todo en Santa Paz.*"

"So you two just keep me informed whenever some *pinche gatos* get you spooked and I'll take care of it like usual." I'm a little embarrassed for talking this way to my *maestro*. Palacios, I couldn't give a fuck about. "I don't need you guys bringing any stinking badges around the neighborhood." Both men smile back at me, but it's not because of my joke. They got me.

Something flickers out the corner of my eye and I turn in time to see the guy curled up in the Suburban wake with a start. He elbows the driver and points at me.

Chapa begins backing toward the doors. "Those men are pointing at you Johnny."

"Really? I think they're looking at you guys." I start down the steps. "Come on, let's go ask them." I hear Chapa and Palacios falling over each other to get through the courthouse doors and I want to smile, but that might cause me to swallow my balls that are firmly lodged in my throat. The Suburban is coming alive as I reach the passenger side and wait for the guy who made me on the steps to lower his window.

"Hey *compadre*, if you guys are here to leave a *consignación* you better take it back to the D.A. because the judge is about to tear you a new ass for trying to ruin his lunch with more work." I lean my head ever so slightly in the window and survey the interior of the vehicle. "Which one of you is the *ciento-tres*?" Two long rifles, AK-47's, front and backseat, and a forth passenger in the back with an Uzi. "The judge will want to talk *con un agente efectivo*."

The guy in the front seat backslaps the driver in the chest signaling him to put the Suburban in motion. "He's on his way." He starts to raise his window. "We'll go get him."

They leave me standing in the middle of the street. I want to piss my pants but my dick is wrapped up around my tongue.

I nose my Crown Victoria around town, taking all the main streets that lead to my Old Man's house. I want to increase the odds of a witness in case I get picked up before I make it home. My rearview mirror shows no sign of the red Suburban or any other car without plates that might be a tail. It's safe enough for lunch, so I make a dogleg before going home.

I head for my girlfriend Cynthia's house. I find her alone in the kitchen stirring a pot of conch-shaped pasta. Her hips sway as she moves the spoon around the pot. I move in behind her and slide my hands around her waist. She lays her head back and nuzzles my neck before she elbows me away. Cynthia turns and reaches into my jacket and pulls out my Browning and lays it on the counter next to the stove.

"I'm hungry."

She pecks me on the lips. "Why else would you come over?"

We eat and I tell her about my day, except for the part where they're following me.

"Poor lions."

"Why so? I haven't said I was going to kill them. I just said they want me to kill 'em."

"Still, if they said you have to kill the lions, then that's what you'll have to do." She clears the dishes. Cynthia's niece comes into the kitchen and hands her a brush and a ribbon. She does the child's hair in a ponytail and tells her to go see what the pig laid. The little girl runs off screaming, "*se van a besar.*" Cynthia comes around the counter and we kiss. Our lips meet and her tongue digs into my mouth and does things I dare not speak for fear I may tip someone off to what I've found.

"You better be careful," she says wiping her mouth.

"What'd I do?"

"With the lions."

"Oh that," I take my gun from Cynthia. "I might just feed them."

"And what if they go crazy after not eating for so long and attack you to get at the food."

"I'll send someone else to feed them."

"Then they'll get killed, and it will be your fault for sending them."

I pull Cynthia toward me and try to steal another kiss but she pushes me away.

"What if they get out and kill a *niño* or some *viejito* who can't run." Cynthia looks at me bug-eyed. "Those lions might even come here."

"Oh, how are they going to come here?"

"I don't know, but what if they do?" Cynthia hugs on my neck.

"I'll come over and spend the night so you won't be scared."

"Okay."

"Really?"

"Sure, if you marry me this evening."

I turn to leave and Cynthia follows me to the door. She looks around for any neighbors who may be spying about. She kisses me long and hard on the mouth.

"I might not be able to come around for a day or two."

"I knew it, always on the weekend. Then I'm going to McAllen tomorrow with my sister." Cynthia holds out her hand.

I reach into my pocket and pinch out a stack of twenties. I rip the paper band and peel off a quarter of the stack. "Get me some socks and underwear."

"You need shirts, and more pants wouldn't hurt either." She keeps her hand out.

"Just the socks and underwear." I kiss her again. "Go in the house, I don't want you outside when I leave."

"You'll come and tell me when you've killed the lions?"

"If I kill the lions." I still haven't said I would.

"Bring me some grease off the lions."

"What the hell for?"

"They say it's good for arthritis, and my Mom's hands have been hurting."

I kiss her one last time and she makes me pay for it by biting my lip. We've been going around for two years. Cynthia has never let me pass second base. I go to whores to get laid. But whores won't give me what Cynthia gives me no matter how much extra I offer to pay. Cynthia kisses me on the mouth and feeds me lunch. There's not a whore in all the *Zona Roja* who would do that for me.

I cruise the four blocks that make up my neighborhood before I pull up to my father's house. I see no out-of-place cars in front of my house or down my block. I turn down my father's street and it's barren. I usually come from work and find a horde of children entrenched in a hot game of street soccer, but not now. I make another round and it's the same on every street; there are no children playing or women sweeping the walk. It's as quiet as Election Day, except for the goats.

Directly in front of our house is a half-acre lot surrounded by a brick fence. Lupín keeps his goats penned there. The animals can't be seen from the street, but their bleating is all that can be heard up and down the block.

I go into my Old Man's house and find it silent except for the sounds coming from the kitchen. El Chaparro sits at the breakfast table stirring dominoes around. Polo the cook wipes down the stove and the tiled countertops, stopping occasionally to look out the kitchen window. Toño sits across from el Chaparro running a scrap of torn T-shirt over an AK-47. These three men and a seventy-two-year-old night watchman are all my Old Man left me to work with in his absence.

El Chaparro selects a hand of dominoes from the spread and begins a game of solitaire. "Did you eat lunch already?"

I take a beer from the fridge and start to go over the phone messages listed on a pad. The list is short. The first two callers are regulars, Homar and el Tarta. They want to move something, and since nothing can move right now, they can wait. The third guy on the list is Juan Ríos, the chief of the Hidalgo PD. He probably wants to know when work will start up again like the other guys, but since I might have to "*brincar el charco*" and lay low on the American side for a while, I make a mental note to invite Juan Ríos out later. For a few rounds of drinks and a couple of table dances at a strip joint I can have an official police escort all over the Valley. The only difference between buying an American cop and buying a Mexican cop is that the American cops are a whole lot cheaper.

El Chaparro lays down a domino and claps his hands. "*Estoy incontenible*, that's the fifth game I've beat the devil out of today."

"I'm glad to see you're hard at work."

"So you *can* talk." El Chaparro collects the dominoes.

"I was followed today."

Toño slams a clip into the AK, pulls it back out then checks the action. "What were they driving?"

"A red Suburban." No one seems too impressed by my news. "There were four guys inside."

Polo looks out the kitchen window, stretching to see as far down either side of the street as possible. "T-t-t-there was a blue Marquis parked down the s-s-street up until a h-h-half hour ago." Polo stutters.

I look at el Chaparro and he nods.

"Think they'll try to get past the gates?" I'm not asking anyone in particular.

El Chaparro lifts his shoulders. "They might pick one of us up to try to force your father's hand."

"You think they'll come after me?"

Toño slaps the table. "They'll have to kill me before they can do anything to you, *Compa* Johnny."

Toño hates Feds and *madrinas* even more, and he feels invincible with his AK-47. I'm not sure if I'm glad my Old Man left me Toño.

"Did your tail look official?" el Chaparro asks. "Did you notice any familiar *ciento-tres* in the pack?"

"Nah, just a bunch of *madrinas* tagging along all day." I pull out my 9 and slide it over to Toño and he starts to break the weapon down. "I talked to them."

El Chaparro gives me the look.

"I just gave 'em some bullshit about the judge and they left."

"Don't you know what kind of people you're dealing with here?" El Chaparro takes what's left of my beer and pours it down the sink.

"*B-b-b-estias* Johnny, *bestias salvajes.*" Polo waives a kitchen towel over his head. "These animals don't respect their own mother."

"So what was I supposed to do?"

"Nothing, just sit tight," el Chaparro says.

Polo, from his post at the window, says, "D-d-did they tell you about the lions?"

"How'd you know?"

"*Pinche* goats haven't shut up all day," el Chaparro says.

"Save one of the lions for me to kill, *Compa* Johnny," Toño says.

"How'd you guys know about Chapa and Palacios?"

"They came by earlier saying Lupín wanted something done about the lions," el Chaparro says.

"We told 'em they could probably find you at the *juzgado*."

"You sent 'em to the *juzgado*?"

"Where'd you want me to tell them to go, your girlfriend's house?"

"I don't know, to go fuck themselves." I pace around the kitchen. "I got motherfuckers following me, you guys got more sons of bitches parked outside, and you send me two fucking lawyers who want me to *quebrar* three *pinche* lions that just happen to be penned up in a retired drug dealer's backyard."

"Calm down Chato," el Chaparro says. "We're supposed to keep things quiet while your dad is out of town, right? Well, the lions made noise, now we have to quiet them."

"What are those guys staking out the neighborhood going to say when we open fire on a bunch of cats?"

"What are they going to say when they find out Lupín is so retired he can afford to keep a private zoo?" El Chaparro arranges his dominoes for a new game. "They left you in charge, remember?"

I walk out and don't stop until I'm standing on the curb. Toño follows. He will not leave my side again until I go to sleep and he beds down outside my door. I tell Toño to put the lock on the gate. I start walking up the street. Toño says something while securing the gate but I can't hear him over the bleating of Lupín's goats. Two doors down from my Old Man's house lives a lady who sells soft drinks and snacks from a *cuartito* outside her house. I enter and Toño catches the screen door before it can slam shut behind me. I pull a couple of bottles of *refrescos* from the cooler. Toño uncaps the soda by laying the edge of the bottle cap on the ejection port of his gun barrel. He twists his wrist and the bottle cap flies off with a pop. Doña Jovita, the owner and operator of the little store, looks up from her seat behind the counter and says, "The only customers I've had all day opened their *refrescos* with their guns. I guess people with guns aren't afraid of the lions."

I pull a twenty out of my pocket and lay it on the counter.

Doña Jova picks up the bill and holds it close to her eyes and shakes her head then lays the bill on the counter again. "I don't have change. Why don't you go and shoot those lions so people can leave their homes? I thought those men who came in here earlier were here to shoot the lions, but they just came in and grabbed some sodas and didn't even leave a deposit for the bottles."

"You didn't happen to notice what type of car those men were driving, did you Doña Jova?"

"I don't know nothing about cars. I haven't dared to stick my head out that door all day. I've been sitting behind this counter hearing roars and panicked goats, waiting for the screams of the first Christian those lions eat up *y rogandole a Dios que no sea yo.*"

I push the twenty toward her. "Keep the change Doña, and if those men come back, tell them they owe me for the deposit on their soda bottles."

"That takes care of that." Doña Jova wads up the bill and shoves it into a pocket on her apron. "Who's going to do something about those lions across the street?"

I finish off my soda and place the empty bottle on the counter. "I'll get some food out to the lions in a little bit," I say on my way out. "That'll quiet them so you won't be afraid."

"I'll be here praying those beasts don't make a meal out of you."

Toño joins me on the curb and we both take turns staring down the street to the sky-blue Marquis that is now parked at the end of the block.

"That the same car you guys saw earlier?"

"I told el Chapparro and Polo we should have taken care of these *hijos de puta* before you came home." Toño unbuttons his light jacket and runs his hands over his belt, stopping on his holstered .45 and extra clip case. "Let's go over there and start chambering bullets on those motherfuckers."

Until I see Toño check his weapon and ammunition, I hadn't realized that I'm no longer wearing my jacket. When Toño finished field dressing my Browning, I holstered the gun in the waistband of my pants. I'm standing on the sidewalk with my Browning and four extra clips strapped around my waist in front of God and a car load of fucking *madrinas*.

"What do you say Johnny, *les hechamos candela?*"

"Let's see what they do first." We move down the street and stop at the corner. I'm about to cross when I hear, "Psst, psst, Johnny, hey, Johnny."

I turn to see el Cato—the neighborhood car thief—hiding half his face behind his front door. I start for his house but he waves me off before I can take a step.

"Johnny, are those guys in the Marquis here for me?"

I look down the street to the Marquis idling half a block away and say over my shoulder, "*Y, ya valió madre*, I think you're fucked."

"*Ay, mamacita.* I swear I haven't even stolen a hubcap for months. Do something for me, Johnny. You know I'm good for it." Cato slams his door shut and I hear locks tumbling. The joke helps ease the knot in my stomach.

We cross the street and make our way around the corner with the blue Marquis following *a vuelta de rueda* behind us. At Lupín's main gate, Toño and I wait for Jaime to let us in while the Marquis parks down the street just enough to be able to watch the entrance.

Jaime is a young man with big ears. He looks like the guy from *Mad Magazine* and I told him so once but all he understood was that I thought he looked like some guy from a magazine. He has thought I'm a *joto* ever since and smiles coquettishly every time he sees me. I brush past Jaime and make my way to the shade of a *palapa* where Leonel, Lupín's half brother is sitting with his shirt unbuttoned and a hundred dollar bill brimming with cocaine resting on his potbelly. Leonel sees me and fills the tip of a butterknife with a mound of coke and sniffs hard. Small specs of coke fall on his bare chest and the scaly gleam from the drug glistens despite the shade.

"I was wondering when someone would come around and help me destroy this evidence." Leonel hands me the bill and butterknife.

I fill the tip with a generous mound and sniff and repeat this motion twice for each nostril before passing the bill on to Toño. "Destroying evidence, is that what we're calling it now?"

"Well hell, if the Feds are going to be rude enough to raid us, I'm not going to share any of this crap with them." Leonel receives the butterknife and bill from Toño and starts stabbing at the coke. "I'm going to finish this shit off, and then I'm taking this hundred dollars to the *Zona* and giving it to the first whore who can get my cock straight." Leonel does another bump of coke. "Fuck the Feds, fuck the lions, fuck Lupín, fuck everybody." I take a pack of cigarettes out of Leonel's shirt pocket and give one to Toño.

"Yeah, fuck everybody 'cept you, *mi Johnny*."

"What about the lions?"

"What?"

"You said fuck the lions. What about 'em?"

"Oh, them, aren't you going to kill 'em?" Leonel takes off his cap and wipes the sweat off his bald head. "Lupín tried to sell those lions to a guy from a circus. Give me three thousand dollars for all three, he says. I'll give you two, the circus guy says. Fuck you, I'll see them dead first. Don't anyone ever feed 'em again Lupín says and leaves for *Valles*. Lupín said you were going to kill 'em. Palacios said you were going to kill 'em. Everybody said, so fuck the lions and good riddance."

"Just like that Leonel, I kill them ¿*y ya*? Can't we just start feeding 'em Lupín's goats or something?" My jaws are starting to clench from the coke.

"*Cállate*, those goats are like Lupín's children. Why do you think Lupín wants the lions dead? He's afraid they might get out and finish off his herd. His own brother's here with those *pinche bestias salvajes*, and Lupín's worried about a herd of goats."

"A car full of *madrinas* followed us over here," I say. "Hell, there might even be Feds outside the gate right now."

"Blue car, with four fuckers inside?"

"Yeah."

"Fuck them. They've been cruising around here all day. If they were going to do something they would've done so by now."

I take another hit of cocaine and Leonel's reasoning starts to ring solid. Fucking Feds are just like the bullies I encountered in grade school back in the States. Them big white boys would come up and promise me an ass kicking after class. But I could never stand the thought of someone laughing while I shat all over myself waiting to get beat down. It's always better to attack a bully and be done with it than to be agonizing slowly over impending doom.

"Let's take a look at them cats" I say, and we start across the large patio and parking area to a remote corner on the lot. Halfway across the lot, the stench of urine and sweat and shit starts to get thick. We have to cover our noses before we reach the lion's den.

The lions are penned in a horse stable. The only opening in the block structure is nailed shut with forklift pallets all the way to the top of the door way. I look through the slits in the pallets and in the shadows I see three sets of yellow-green eyes, sunken deep in their sockets, staring back at me.

The male lion, the youngest and smallest in size of the three cats, lies on its stomach with its chin resting on outstretched paws near the doorway. The two she lions, their pelts sagging off their skeletal frames, watch us from the shadowy corners of the stable, staying out of the rays of light that stream through the slits of the makeshift cage door. They cringe in the gray darkness.

These animals have been cared for up until now. They've been fed regularly, and instead of learning how to hunt and fend for themselves, the three lions have learned—through days and years of experiencing the snub of the chain, the unyielding bars—their limitations and the role humans play in their lives. Now that the humans are no longer the food givers, the lions watch from the shadows and remember their natural instincts. Their eyes look out through the wooden bars, watchful, alert, waiting for the keeper to forget the door, for the collar to fray, the bar to loosen.

I look at Toño and he nods back at me. I pull my gun and sit down cross-legged two paces in front of the boarded-up doorway. I set my sights on a one-and-a-half-inch square hole in the base of the wooden pallet that exposes the male lion's forehead. I drop the safety and the 150-lb baby lion lifts its head a fraction. I squeeze off a shot and a blue-black hole appears instantly on the lion's forehead. Its lifeless head lands on the now limp outstretched paws. I want to take a moment and contemplate this blue-black hole that's screaming the reality of my actions back at me, but there's no time. There never is.

Toño rushes the door and pumps two bullets from his .45 through the wooden slits. His shots are quick and his aim off. The she-lions bounce off the walls in a wild frenzy. I don't know if they are incensed over the gunfire or if it's the blood trickling out of the male lion's mouth and forehead. Nothing can be heard over the shrieks and roars of the she-lions. I motion for Toño to follow my lead. Toño steps out of my way. I go forward looking down the sights of my gun. I get close enough to the doorway to feel the breeze from the lioness's fanning swipes. I take aim through the wooden bars and pull my trigger three times. The shots send the she-lions to the back of the stable. Toño appears beside me and takes aim and fires. The cat's chin hits the concrete floor hard and slides across the pen clearing a path through the dust and debris. The lioness raises its head groggily and lunges for the door. I open fire and knock the beast back to a sitting position. Toño and I alternate our attacks on the lions like wolves in a pack. As soon as I finish my volley, Toño steps ahead of me and draws a bead on the other she-lion. He hits her square on the forehead. The lion's head swings from side to side then comes crashing down to the base of the doorway next to the limp body of the male lion.

I motion Toño back and we change clips as we regroup then move forward behind our guns. The last lion is hunched back in a far corner of the stable. I take aim and fire. The bullet hits the she-lion in the neck just below her jaw. The shot tumbles her over backward. I lower my aim to survey the damage. The lioness, struck and wounded, with only a fraction of an instant to rally, lunges, toward us not with blind rage, but with all the deliberate intention of destruction. She concentrates her lunge on the top corner of the doorway. The wooden pallet yields under the lioness's rush and slaps the concrete frame. Toño's Colt spits fire and the she-lion falls on its back. It regains its footing and slinks into a corner. The big cat is panting heavily and repeatedly coughing up bubbled globs of blood that flow over its chin and down its chest.

The shot is awkward. I have to lean against the building and aim sideways through the doorway. I draw a bead and fire. The lion's head crashes against the block wall then falls to the floor with a thud. I wave my hand over my head to signal she's dead and step away from the doorway. I haven't brought my foot down for the second step when a sudden gust sends the stagnant coppery breath of the she-lion down the back of my neck. I turn in time to see the outstretched body of the she-lion sailing through the air toward the sagging pallet at the top of the doorway. I turn and squeeze off shots indiscriminately. Toño is to one side of me emptying his .45 into the lion. El Chaparro appears and fires a pump action .22 from my left flank into the stable. The lion claws the top portion of the barred doorway with open mouth and guttural shrieks then falls dead next to the other two lions lying on the floor.

El Chapparro prods the lions with the barrel of the .22 and makes sure they are dead. Leonel and Jaime busy themselves tearing down the wooden pallets from the doorway. This proves easy as the loosened concrete nails break away and the wooden pallets splinter with only a few whacks of an axe.

Ropes are slipped around the lions' necks and their carcasses are dragged out of the stable. During the shooting I hadn't noticed the group of people that gathered within the patio. Someone pulls out a camera and we take turns posing with the dead lions. Knives and other cutting instruments are produced and el Chapparro, Leonel, Jaime, and some others begin skinning the lions.

El Chapparro wraps his stubby fingers around one of the lion's ears and begins sawing off its snout with a hacksaw.

"What are you doing that for?"

El Chapparro tears off the lion's lower jaw and holds it up to me. "Palacios and Chapa say they have a jeweler who'll pay 250 dollars for every fang and 150 dollars for each claw."

An abacus goes off in my mind, and then I do what every man should do when he realizes he's been duped. I negotiate two claws, a fang, and a jar of what ever grease they can get off the lions to take to Cynthia for her mother.

I signal Toño for us to leave. Toño secures the film from the guy snapping off the pictures then comes trotting after me. We make our way past the main gate through a crowd that yells and cheers us as we pass. A group of red-faced happy children trail after us. I've never hit one out of the park in the bottom of the ninth. I've never sunk one at the buzzer, never intercepted for a touchdown, never played a guitar solo, never been asked to address the crowd other than to give an alibi, so this is it for me. I reek of cat urine and gunpowder but every woman on the block is gushing over me, their children are elbowing each other for a chance to touch me, and the men are being pushed into the deepest darkest parts of their wives' and kids' hearts to make room for me and they go without protest, nodding their recognition of this thing I've done that no one else could do. My ears ring from the gunfire and shouting kids. The smell of cat piss and decay has penetrated my clothes and it's hard to catch my breath as I wade through the sea of extended hands clamoring to pump mine.

Over the smiling faces of the children, at the other end of the block, a sky blue Marquis sits idling.

The occupants stare at the scene through the windshield, watchful, alert, waiting for the keeper to forget the door, for the frayed collar, the loosened bar, waiting for their chance to lunge, waiting.

Chapter XIV

I don't mind being tailed that much—I mean, being followed is a lot better than being picked up by the *federales*. Sure, it's a little embarrassing, but I think every law student should show up to school with a Suburban full of *federales* on his tail every now and then, just so the rest of the class knows what kind of game they're getting into. It's all the sneaking and hiding just to do simple chores like study for an exam that really sucks about being hunted by the Feds.

I have to ditch the Crown Victoria at the gas station where Pecas works. Every cop in town knows my car. This was a good thing when it came to getting out of tickets or parking with Cynthia without being bothered. But lately I've been heading a parade of cops through the streets of Reynosa. El Conejo will take my car to the *juzgado* so the guns tailing me will think I'm inside working. Fucking car is almost brand new and I have to trust it to a kid who can barely see over the dashboard. I hide in the bathroom till Pecas finishes his shift, chainsmoking my last four Raleighs to keep from gagging on the smell of shit and urine mixed with *Fabuloso* cleaner.

We walk down the railroad tracks away from the Gasolinera Ramírez toward La Canta Ranas. Pecas hits each tie in stride, but I have to single step to avoid falling headlong on the tracks.

Pecas sticks his chin out and says, "When we reach the end of that fence, I'll take a look behind us. If I take off running, you follow."

"I know."

"Don't stop."

"I know."

"Even if they call you, '*Ay chavo, ven.*'"

"I say, '*ven por mi*,' and keep running. I know."

We reach the fence and I say a silent prayer while Pecas sneaks a peak. "There's a truck, Johnny. I can't tell what kind of cops. But I don't think they're Feds."

The Feds *me pusieron campana,* have hung a cowbell on me. This is how we say that the Feds have let the word slip that they're after me. Now the Feds don't have to tail me round the clock anymore. If they want to know where I'm at, all they have to do is find the nearest guy with a badge and ask. There's a job with the Feds waiting for any cop who'll give me up. A reward has been put on my ass.

We round the fence and go down a narrow walk that zigzags between the cinderblock rooms where whores used to bring their clients back when La Canta Ranas was part of the red-light district. There's no furniture in these rooms except for the bare essentials, a bed, some type of stove or hot plate sitting on a tin table, maybe a dresser and an ice chest, and of course a radio. There's music spilling from the open doors, and every radio is tuned to high and on a different station. Women sit at their windows in open robes, towels wrapped around their heads, looking into handheld mirrors, plucking eyebrows or penciling in moles over their lips while their kids run around in saggy diapers on bare concrete floors screaming louder than the radio.

Everyone tries to hold their shit together in the *vecindad.* The men stand around doorways drinking *caguamas* and smoking pot, nodding our recognition as we make our way through the *vecindad* with a flicker of eye contact, screaming in that one glance all the hate and sadness and loneliness, all the want and got-to-have, all the *ah huevos*, and then the eyes go out, cast down again, slinking back into their sockets so as not to roll out with the next nod. I'm with Pecas—and Pecas has a rep as a guy who *se da un tiro*, will fight if need be—so all I have to do is stay grim and nod in return and just keep walking past the clumps of tattooed men through the maze of narrow walkways and alleys that even cops avoid.

My whole world's a *vecindad.*

We pile our books on Pecas's table and get ready to study. I take out a bag of weed and start breaking up buds on the front page of *El Día.* I have no rolling papers or cigarettes so Pecas goes to his backdoor and whistles. A lanky kid about 14 years old named Omar comes running to his call.

"Omar, go to the *deposito* and buy us a pack of cigarettes."

I pull out a 50,000 peso bill. "Tell him to buy some Raleighs and to keep the change."

"Hear that, *buey*? Your going to make some cash so don't take forever."

Pecas opens a *Código de Procedimientos Penal* and starts thumbing through the pages. We have final exams before we graduate. If we pass these tests, we'll be eligible to take the bar exam and become licensed attorneys. Pecas paces up and down his kitchen reciting from memory, "*Los siete elementos del delito son la tipicidad, antijuricidad—*"

The night my grandfather died, I could hear my Old Man whimpering. He's sitting in a corner sniffling, but I can't tell if he's crying or if it's just the coke. He keeps ordering his *pistoleros* to play the same song on the stereo over and over, "*Mi viejo, mi querido viejo,*" by José Alfredo Jiménez. He doesn't look as tough as he usually does. He looks old and tired and scared.

Now we're in California for my grandfather's funeral. I can see my brothers and sister huddled around our mother sobbing uncontrollably. My Old Man's walking down the aisle to where the casket housing my grandfather's body lies. My Old Man fights every step, swinging a half-empty bottle of J&B ahead of him, but the pine box pulls him along. When he gets close enough to peer in—it's like a grenade has gone off and my Old Man reels back dropping the whiskey bottle to shield his face with trembling hands. I'm standing, ashamed for crying, when I start getting shaken. It's my Old Man and he has me by the shoulders, his face drawn close to mine, tears are streaming down our faces, and he keeps saying, "*Se me murió el gusto.*"

I blink then see my Dad on top of a tractor wiping sweat from his neck. I'm little and can't ride with him because I might fall and get chewed up by the disk blades. When he gets back to the truck, I help him off with his rubber boots. I have a clear image of thin pale ankles being choked by white socks that were calf-length when I watched him put them on that morning.

Now I see my Old Man walking chained at the hips and ankles through the halls of the Brownsville courthouse. He walks straight, his chin jutting out, but he refuses to meet my gaze. I sidestep next to him, the chains clanking along the marble floor echoing throughout the corridor, but my Old Man walks on with eyes fixed ahead and never turns toward me.

"It's Omar, Johnny."

Omar comes in and throws the pack of cigarettes on the table then grabs a *Código Civil*.

"What you guys looking at these books for?" Omar asks then starts going through the *Código* page by page.

"You're not studying, Johnny," Pecas says. "*Andas sacado de onda*, right? You can't concentrate."

"Hey, these books don't have any pictures, no drawings, nothing, just a bunch of writing," Omar says.

"They're not comic books. Those are law books, we're going to be lawyers," I say.

"But not even a drawing, a *pinche* graph, anything? The books at my school all have pictures and drawings, graphs, maps. What happened to these books?"

"They're not those kind of books."

"*Tira al león*, Johnny. Don't bother with him. He's just a kid. He don't know," Pecas says. "No sense in worrying about getting picked up. That it's going to happen is a sure bet. You guys got too big. Me, I'm small time. If I see that things get too hot I'll let myself get caught stealing something, a radio or some ornament off a car. I'd rather get beat by the municipal cops than the Feds . . ."

He's right. I can't read or study law right now; my mind is off somewhere else, *costeando*, off walking some distant shore. There's a newspaper on the table, so I start looking over the headlines while Pecas talks. *Detienen al Kino en Tampico* is the big news of the day. The story reads that el Kino, head of the national Pemex union, was found in possession of a large cache of weapons— the paper doesn't bother to say *why* a union leader would have hundreds of assault rifles. According to the paper, there was a shootout during the arrest and a federal D.A. got killed before they could get to el Kino. I've met el Kino on several occasions and that little runt of a man being in a shootout with the Feds is as likely as the kids from Menudo being straight. There're pictures of the weapons seized and on another table there're stacks of cash and rows of Rolex watches lined up. I search the stacks of bills to see if I can spot any that I marked while counting, but the picture is too grainy. The paper says this is all part of the new President's war on corruption, but I know that Salinas is taking out everyone who can tie him to the fixed election.

I read further down the paper and see that *comandante* Torres del Rey's resignation as *primer comandante* has been made official. So there goes our cover. In another story, the new President is congratulating Culeroni for his heroic battle against organized crime. I almost shit my pants when I read further and learn that the praise is coming for apprehending Don Celestino in Guadalajara. The paper doesn't say when or how Don Celestino got picked up or who was with him when it happened. Fucking Culeroni is getting praised from the President when everyone in Reynosa knows that that son of a bitch is the only one who has been able to move shit across the border since the inauguration. Fucking papers twist the shit out of everything. They tell the story all right, but they get it backward. It's like some horrible version of history where the white people are the good guys. Fucking Don Beto and Don Felix, those fuckers own the newspapers. They could print the truth. They could write what everyone already knows, that the cops are the real organized crime and that all we do is fight for a chance to pay them off. Shit, I learned not to trust the papers way back during the *pesera* wars.

I turn to the *Sección Policiaca* and see a picture of Tavo Hasso being loaded into a police car.

"Tavo Hasso got brought in for sentencing the other day," I say to Pecas as I slide the newspaper in front of him.

"Seven years. It's all around the neighborhood," Pecas says matter-of-factly.

"What do you think's going to happen to me? You think I'll come out in the papers?"

"For what? Culeroni and the guys following you?"

"Yeah."

"You're going to get picked up, beaten. If you're lucky, you can cut a deal. If not, they'll lock you up or kill you."

"Fuck you."

"What? You asked."

"Yeah, but I didn't ask for you to condemn me. What the fuck did I ever do to deserve to get tortured and shit?"

"You're guilty, Johnny. You're in on everything. You're part of it."

"Part of what, paying off cops? The only thing I'm guilty of is not being one of them."

"Complain now if you want, but I never heard you bitch about driving around in that fancy car with your pockets stuffed with money."

"You guys have eleven books, and not one of them has any pictures or drawings," Omar says.

So this is the way it is. Even Pecas is singing *Who's Crying Now?* Fucking Pecas, of all people he should know that I couldn't give a crap about the cars and money. I just care about . . . I just care about—my Old Man. I'm not a pussy or anything, it's just that people don't understand; a guy has to look out for his Old Man or he isn't shit. Fuck, every *corrido* I've ever heard says that's the way it is.

"Eleven books, and not one has any pictures," Omar says.

"I'm nothing compared to you. I'll get off with a few slaps. Maybe miss a few days of school. You? Shit, who knows what they'll do to you," Pecas says.

"Or to you, if they find out you've been selling weed for me," I say.

"If they're following you, they'll pick you up. *Esa 'sta fácil*," Omar says.

"Maybe you shouldn't come around here anymore, Johnny," Pecas says.

Pecas and I sit across from each other, neither one of us able to look the other in the eye. Omar raises a *Código Penal* over his head and hurls it to the ground breaking the silence, "*Estos libros no sirven pa' nada, son puras palabras.*"

They posted our grades on a bulletin board and Pecas passed his exams with better scores than mine, but he hasn't come to school since we took the tests.

The director of our campus came into our classroom to explain how we won't get our degrees until we fill out an application and pay a fee, and of course pass the *examen profesional*. Then he announces the winner of the best student award. It goes to this lady who just started working at the *juzgado*.

"That's bullshit," I whisper under my breath but loud enough for Dávila sitting next to me to hear.

"They only gave it to her because she got the job at the *juzgado*," Dávila says. "Hey, you work at the *juzgado*, why didn't they give you the award?"

"Pecas should've got that award. He got better grades than all of us."

"They're not going to give an award to a *mariguano*," Dávila says.

After class I head over to Cynthia's house. We sit and talk on her porch. My graduation only means one thing to her, but I've got other things on my mind.

"Hey, my sister might come out. And don't play dumb. I said you graduated," she says wrestling out of my arms.

"Not yet. I still have to pass the bar exam. We haven't even had the ceremony."

"That's nothing. You'll pass the exam and you'll buy me a dress for the dance. You've graduated, now when are you coming to talk to my father?" she asks rubbing up against me.

"About what?" I act dumb.

"I'm going to walk back in if you don't cut it out. Maybe your *Licenciada* friends at the *juzgado* can explain what I'm talking about when you tell them at work tomorrow that you've passed all your tests."

"You mean about us getting married? I told you, I still have to pass the bar and I need to save more money." I don't bother to mention that I might get picked up before I even get to take the fucking exam.

"You've got a house and a degree. If you want a wife to go along with that, you better do something quick or I will."

"What are you going to do, come talk to *my* Old Man?"

"You do something or I will. Just think about that."

"Just think about that," she says. I think the shit out of everything. "Think about that," she says. Fuck, that's all I do is think about *that.*

My Old Man came back to Reynosa about a month after my graduation, just in time for his birthday. He rents out the Salón Jade and sends for bands. He spends the days before his birthday calling everyone in town, but the night of the party the hall is empty except for my immediate family and the musicians and the *pistoleros*. It's not like my Old Man misses the company because he's in the bathroom with his *pistoleros* snorting coke anyway. I hammer whiskey highballs with my brothers and sister while their kids run around the dance floor. By ten o'clock we're all back at my Old Man's house drunk and eating steaks off of silver platters with our fingers.

My brothers, sister, and their kids stay over at the house for a few days after the party. It's cool hanging out around the pool—smoking weed, and exchanging stories about when we were kids—until I ask them about the club they opened in McAllen.

"What do you mean you lost the club? It's a fucking building. How do you lose a fucking building?"

"The building's still there. We just can't get into it anymore," my oldest brother Chilo says.

"They changed the locks when we fell behind on the rent," Rubén says.

"How the hell did you guys fall behind on the rent? I heard there were people lined up all around the building waiting to get in every weekend. You must've been making some money."

"Well, it's expensive to run a club," Chilo says.

"Yeah, Johnny. You don't know. You just can't show up to your own club dressed in rags," Lourdes says.

"But what about all that stuff you bought? The hundred thousand dollar light and sound system, the custom stage?"

"You're such a dumb-ass, Johnny," Lourdes says. "They don't let you take that stuff out. Besides, who cares about losing that shit—we're rich."

Two shots sound off from inside the house. By the time we reach the back door, two more shots go off. My Old Man's sitting at the dining table with his *pistoleros* listening to those musicians from the *Huasteca* who play violins and mandolins. The phone is propped in front of my Old Man and next to it there's a bent hundred dollar bill with coke spilling out of it. The guy who plays the harp is on one knee with his pants pulled up, blood trickling down his shin.

"What the hell's going on? Junior asks.

"He just caught some shrapnel," my Old Man says pointing with his still smoking .38 at the wounded harp player.

"What were you shooting at?" Lourdes asks.

"I just squeezed off a couple of rounds at the floor *por el gusto de vivir*. C'mon join me. Somebody serve some more whiskey."

"And you didn't think the bullets would bounce off the floor?" I ask.

"Yeah, after this *pendejo* got hit. That's why I shot the next two into the ceiling."

"You shot into the ceiling, Dad, our kids are up there," Rubén says. "Michael, Chris!"

My nieces and nephews come running down the stairs with their eyes about to bulge out of their sockets. My Old Man takes a look at his grandkids and busts out laughing.

"Hey look, *se asustaron*."

"Why's grandpa shootin' people?" my nephew, Chris, cries.

My sisters-in-law start yelling about leaving and everyone packs up their shit and loads up cars so they can cross back over to the States. I run upstairs to my parents' room to look for my mom. There are ceiling tiles and cellophane wrapping thrown around the room. My mom is stuffing stacks of money down her denim dress.

"What are you doing?"

"Oh, Johnny, good it's you. I don't want you to let anyone in my room while I'm gone."

"Where are you going?"

"I'm going to go stay with your sister in Edinburg for a while until your dad settles down."

"What are you going to do with all that money?"

My mom's eyes start to rim with tears. She stomps her foot raising her arms like Scarlett O'Hara in *Gone With the Wind*, only with a stack of money in each clenched fists instead of carrots, and says, "Why can't I take a little something for me? I can't stay around your father anymore. He shot up every hotel we stayed at while we were down south. You know what it's like getting room service brought to a bullet-riddled room? It's embarrassing, that's what it's like. I deserve something for all I've had to put up with. What about me? Nobody ever considers me. What about me?"

I go back downstairs and watch my brothers, sister, their kids, and my mom load up into their cars and drive away. I go back in the house and my Old Man's got the band playing again. He smiles when he sees me.

"All those worthless fuckers leave already?"

"You mean your family? Yeah, they're gone."

My Old Man points his .38 at the band and says, "Good, now all I got to worry about is not shooting one of these guys. Hey, let me make a few calls and I'll get a bunch of whores to fly up from the D.F. You be ready to pick them up at the airport."

"What do you want to be shooting in the house for?" I say. "You're going to send for whores, now, when we have all this heat? What's wrong with the whores around here?"

"You gonna start giving me shit? You shoot up the whole neighborhood killing lions and you want to give me shit? You can abandon me like everyone else if you're gonna start giving me shit. Your pussywhipped brothers. Your whore sister. Your money-hungry Mom. Even *el pinche puto del* Chaparro is abandoning me. I can't get anyone to pick up the phone. You're not any different. You didn't pull your gun that time I shot it out with Lolo. You just stood there."

"I didn't have a gun."

"You have one now. You gonna pull it when they come for me? *Qué chingados.* You're gonna run just like that black jackrabbit, el *Chorty*, did. Thirty years of riding together and he abandons me. *No vale madre ese puto.* But just wait and see. Just wait. I've helped a lot of people in this town. And if el *pinche puto de* Culeroni comes around here, everyone will rise up for me. Just wait, you'll all see."

"Where's el Chaparro?"

"Turning himself in, the *pendejo.* If you hurry you can watch him drag his ass down the street. I didn't let him take a car."

I run outside and out the main fence. El Chaparro is about fifty meters from the corner. It takes me a minute to catch my breath once I reach him. "Where you going, *Chorty?* My Old Man said you're turning yourself in. Who you turning yourself in to? You haven't done anything."

"My oldest called about an hour ago. The Feds were at my house saying they had a warrant for my arrest. They slapped my boy around. They didn't have to hurt my boy—I'm the one they're looking for."

"But for what?"

"For that load I lost in Nayarit."

"But that was a while back, and we fixed that one."

"We had it fixed as long as Torres del Rey was *comandante.*"

"But can't Torres del Rey call someone? He still must have friends working for the Feds."

"Friends are only friends when you have something they want. Besides, Torres can't help anyone from the grave."

"El *comandante* Torres is dead?"

"Probably, he was kidnapped two days ago from his apartment in Mexico City. You hadn't heard?"

"No, the papers didn't say shit about that, just about him resigning."

"Yeah, well, he's gone now."

"Hey, let me get my car and I'll drive you over to Chayo's. He'll have you on the other side before morning."

"You want me to run? No, Chato, there's no use running from anything. All you end up doing is running into something worse and then pretty soon all you got is trouble behind you and trouble ahead. I'll go and turn myself in to the Feds and maybe they'll keep it down to a few mineral waters up my nose."

"Shit, Chaparro, how'd everything get so fucked up? We were supposed to be sitting pretty, raking in cash once the new President took office. Bald motherfucker's been in office a month and all we are is fucked."

"Don't complain, Chato. Can you imagine what your dad would've been like if he had succeeded in buying the Presidency?"

"He'd sit on a mountain of coke in the middle of the *Zócalo*. Man that shit's made him crazy."

"It's the money that made him crazy, not the coke. You know, that's the only thing that could've ever parted me and your dad, money."

"Maybe we should hole up with my Old Man and figure out some way to get Culeroni before he gets us. We could pay someone to take him out."

"And then what? Live for the next shootout? We got into this business to make money, not to kill people. The first guy I ever shot cost me only two pesos. I blew his face off with a shotgun and left him lying in some reeds by a river. A cop stopped me before I could get a hundred meters from the body and said hunting was prohibited this close to town. I gave him a two peso *mordida* and he let me go. When they found the body later, I know the cop must have figured it was me but he couldn't say shit without having to explain why he had let me go in the first place. Two fucking pesos. How much you think a man's life's worth, Chato?"

El Chaparro hugs me right there on the street. When he finally lets go, he says, "Take some money to my family later if you can, but what you got to do right now is take whatever you got and jump over to the other side. Get your girlfriend and get yourself across the border right now."

"I don't think she'll go without us being married."

"Then you leave without her. You got to let her go if she won't follow. You don't even want to think about what'll happen if those guys on your tail pick you up while you're with her. Go away, Chato. Go away now or be ready to take what comes alone. Go to the States."

"You know I can't do that." I imagine my fate slowly. "Maybe they'll write a *corrido* about me."

"Now you sound like Julio Cortina's son." We walk off in opposite directions with the sun blazing overhead and the sounds of *Huasteca* music filling the empty street.

I don't bother to go back in the house. Dad's all coked-up. I have to go to a pharmacy and buy a few boxes of Rohypnol. Roofies are the best for coming down from coke. I think the Roche Company made them especially for coming down from coke; I mean, what else can people use roofies for anyway? I'll drop a few pills into my Old Man's whiskey and try to get him in bed so at least he can be sober if any shit comes down.

I pay the guy behind the counter at the pharmacy fifty U.S. for five boxes of Rohypnol. My rearview mirror is empty when I start the car again so I figure it's safe for me to pay Cynthia a visit. Before I get off the Crown Victoria at Cynthia's house, I tear open a box of roofies and drop a couple of pills on my tongue. They immediately dissolve and before I can get across the driveway, I feel myself downshift and the whole world goes into slow motion.

Cynthia comes to the kitchen door, takes one look at me, and like a crazy woman grabs my face and starts lifting my eyelids.

"Look at you," Cynthia slurs out of wavy lips. "Don't you have enough problems that you have to walk around with a face like an idiot too?"

"That's what I needed to tell you. I have these problems and my Old Man—and I can't go to Pecas's house—it's just a matter of time and I don't want to be around you then so you better find someone else," I say and walk back to the car.

I hear Cynthia cry, "Johnny, wait, *no me dejes.*" And right there it hits me. Like I say, the whole world is in slow motion and things get real clear real fast when a guy can take a slow look. The reason you can't win is that fucking up happens instantaneously. There's never a chance to slow down and take notice that every step has been fucked up from the word go, no matter how good of an idea it seemed to be at the time because every decision has been based on fear or need.

The trip home seems to take a lot longer than usual. I stop at a *deposito* and buy a case of Coronas, two cartons of Raleighs, chips, peanuts, mineral water, and some *carne seca.* I drop two more roofies and gulp down half a beer when I pull up to my house—I can still hear the music spilling over from the next block. I spend the rest of the day nodding off in front of the TV. I wake up in a dark house and I'm hungry so I start frying up some eggs and *carne seca.* A pair of headlights shines through the kitchen window. It's el Compadrito and Toño. I open the front door before they can knock.

"The *feos* have just busted into your father's house," Compadrito says. "I was on the way to take Toño here to the bus station when we see a convoy of Suburbans heading straight for your father's house."

"They came off their Suburbans with AK's at the ready, *mi Johnny,*" Toño says. "Give me a gun so I can go save *el jefe.*"

"Was there any shooting coming from inside the house?"

"You could hear things crashing around and people yelling—I think I heard your dad cussing—we didn't hear any shooting. We didn't stop or anything, just kind of rolled by slow," Compadrito says. "What should we do, *jefecito*?"

"Get Toño to the bus station so he can go home, and then you jump to the other side and go to my sister's house and tell my Mom and everyone not to come across till I say it's okay."

"Johnny, I can't go to Sinaloa now," Toño says. "I've got to stay and even the score for your dad."

"There's nothing we can do against the Feds, there's too many of 'em. Just go back home and when things cool down, I'll send for you."

"No, Johnny, you don't understand. Beto was leading the convoy that raided your dad's house," Toño says.

"You sure? You got a good look?"

"He was leaning over in his truck, biting his fingernails the way he always does. I saw him just as plain as I see you now."

"It was Beto, Johnny," el Compadrito says. "It was his truck. He was driving, and fifteen Suburbans filled with *feos* stretched out behind him. How could Beto do this to us? He knows I have kids to feed."

"*Compa* Johnny, are you going to jump over to the other side?"

"No, I'm not going anywhere."

I go into my closet and unlock a dresser drawer and start pulling out stacks of money. There's a black and silver Olympia typewriter lying in a corner of the closet. I remember buying it with the first *mordida* I got after I started working in the *juzgado*, figuring I'd practice my typing and move up the ranks to a *secretarios*' position—another plan that didn't work out. Inside the case there're some pens, carbon paper, whiteout, and a ream of paper. I take everything out and bounce them on the bed, typewriter and all. I scoop up all the money and fill the typewriter case and carry it back outside.

"Here, there's about fifty thousand—forty-eight thousand, seven hundred and twenty to be exact. You better not touch a fucking penny."

El Compadrito grabs the case and gets on the truck. Toño stands in front of me and says, "I'll stay with you if you want me to."

"The Feds will be busy for the rest of the night at my Old Man's house. Then who knows how long they'll take working him over. Maybe I can get some help from the judge tomorrow. If not, I'll stick it out for a while to see how things look. I'll have time to get away."

"You know I'm only going because I have something to settle with Beto or else I wouldn't leave, even if you ordered me to," Toño says.

"Get that out of your head, I know Beto would never cross us," I lie. I don't have time to explain to Toño how complicated this is; I need him to leave. When the Feds show up, I don't need anyone around who'll give them an excuse to start shooting. I don't want Toño to start taking wild shots—like he did when we killed the lions—and start a firefight.

I go back in my house and start gathering up everything that might incriminate me. I pull out all of my weed and start rolling. I have about forty joints when I finish. I get out two ziplock baggies full of coke—this is the coke I had left over from what I had split with Toño after my Old man's last party a year ago. I dump the coke out on a plate. I use my knife to separate a few quarter inch thick lines and snort these up. I tear open all the boxes of roofies and push the pills out of their strip and into an ashtray. I look at my kitchen with the table covered by a pile of joints, a plate full of coke, an ashtray that looks more like a candy dish now that it's full of roofies, beer bottles on the counters, cigarettes smoking in the ashtray, and *machacado con huevo* burning on the stove. A real *mariguano* buffet.

I pull my 9mm and start to take it apart. I strip the gun down and scatter all the pieces except for the recoil spring. This I take to the backyard and throw it over the fence—a guy can't be charged with carrying a fire arm if it doesn't fire. When I get back in, I do a few more lines and drop a couple more roofies then I start going around the house again checking for anything I might have missed. There's the typewriter lying on my bed. I take the machine back to the kitchen and make space for it on the table next to the drugs. I load the machine with paper and then pull the plate over and do two lines up each nostril. I light a joint and sit back and think. I think way back, as far as I can. There was something. I'd just met Cynthia for the first time and there was drinking and singing. I was happy. I start hammering away at the typewriter. The keys snap like hail on concrete. The sound is not as bad as gunfire, but just as nerve-wracking.

By morning, I've typed over forty pages. I drop a couple more roofies to unlock my jaws and then I place a call to the *juzgado* and ask to speak with the judge.

"What are you doing calling here?" the judge says.

"Have you heard about my dad?" I light a joint.

"It's all over the newspaper. You can't work here anymore."

"Are you going to help him?"

"Yes, I'm going to write an *Auto Formal de Prisión* so flimsy a first-year law student could stumble through it. Now hang up and don't call or come around here."

The judge isn't going to help my Old Man. Hell, he probably hasn't even gotten the indictment and already he's talking about declaring my dad formally a prisoner.

I dial every number for every *compadre* my Old Man has and every time I get the same thing on the other end of the line, "*Dile que no estoy.*"

When the sun goes down, I pick up the phone again and dial Richard's number. "Hey? Richard? Listen, you better not go by my Old Man's house. He got raided last night. Stay away from Beto too, he might be a *dedo.*"

I can hear Richard squawk through the receiver, "I knew it. I'm going to—" I hang up before Richard can finish.

I dial one more time and wait for what seems like forever to hear my sister's voice at the other end of the line. "Lourdes?"

"Johnny? What do you want? Hurry, I'm getting ready to go out. It's *baile* time!" she says.

"Dad got busted last night—he's going to get thrown in jail."

"So? What do you want me to do? I'm still going out to the *baile.*"

The phone goes dead before I get a chance to

ask her if el Compadrito had left my typewriter case at her house.

Fuck me. Fuck me. Fuck me. What the fuck can I do? What the fuck have I done? I look at the plate of coke and decide I'm tired of making lines. I clump all the coke in the center of the plate and make a tight spiral away from the mound of coke in the center till I reach the edge of the plate. This way I can do one continuous line till I get to the center before I have to prepare more coke for snorting. This speeds up my writing tremendously.

By the third night I'm almost through with the ream of paper. My fingers are yellow from holding so many cigarettes. I've eaten so many roofies that the coke can hardly keep me awake. I pick up a joint from a pile of the remaining three or four and light it. It dangles from the corner of my mouth as I type. I can see headlights shining through my kitchen window now. There're cars gathering outside. The sun is starting to poke out and its rays color the underbelly of the clouds a deep purple. It's another velvet morning—and I'm not straight. I hear car doors slam and gruff voices, boots stomping pavement. I lick the tip of my joint but my mouth is too dry to make spit. I tug on the joint and listen to the chain snap then rattle off my gate. I hear men running up my walk. There's pounding at my door.

"¿*Quién es*?" I fill my lungs with smoke and hold it through more pounding on the door. The frame is starting to splinter. I exhale.

"¿*Quién es*?"

Epilogue

In the end, I alone survived without being indicted.

El Chano, el Guerro Gil and Beto, and I guess every other second in command from all the other *clickas* screwed over their bosses and bought the Presidency for themselves. Culeroni raided Don Celestino and all of the other organizations, my Old Man's included. The raids were done to show the gringos that the new President was actively participating in the drug war. The newspapers got their headlines. México continued to receive the drug certification money from Uncle Sam for fighting trafficking. But thanks to el Richard, Beto never lived to see his plan bear fruit. Now el Chano has the *plaza* on a national level.

I was held in a 9X6 room where I slept handcuffed on the floor in puddles of my own urine. From the next room I could hear the tortured screams of my father as the Feds worked him over for nine days and nights. At the start of what I could figure to be the tenth day—I received one meal a day—a light-skinned effeminate looking man wearing a pair of those beltless pants came into my cell and introduced himself as *sub-comandante* Villegas. A guy I recognized from the State Police took the cuffs off of me. Villegas coughs after announcing himself, and the guy from the State Police steps up and smashes my teeth in. I start to gag and have to drop to all fours to keep from drowning on my own blood. After a few moments, I'm able to breathe with some regularity and manage to get myself standing.

Villegas reaches into his breast pocket and pulls out a joint which he sticks into my gaping mouth.

"I know all about you," he says in English. "Oh, you thought you were the only kid to grow up around gringos? I speak English and I can read it too."

He raises a flame to the end of the joint and I fill my lungs with smoke. I immediately start to gag again. I spit out clumps of bloody phlegm almost hitting Villegas's shoes.

"Look at you. You look ridiculous," he says. "Almost as ridiculous as all those ramblings we found in your house. You are a *mariguano* driven by vice, and therefore not a word of what you say can be trusted."

I know how that would've been worded had I been indicted: 23 de Febrero 1990, *Continuando con la Campania permanente contra el narcotráfico . . .Juan N. Cortina, en violación al articulo 187 del código penal, se declara adicto a la mariguana . . ."*

I was out an hour after the Feds got word from the judge that I was fired from my job at the courthouse.

My Old Man didn't get off so easy. He was right though, the *mañosos* did rise up against the Feds. But not for him.